"If you call me 'sir' just once more, Kate, I shall strangle you!"

"But of course I must call you 'sir,' Mr. Tait-Bouverie. You forget that I am in your aunt's employ—her housekeeper."

"There are housekeepers and housekeepers, and well you know it. You may cook divinely, but you are no more a housekeeper than I am. I confess that I am curious."

Kate said coolly, "I'm sure that my plans are of no interest to you, s... Mr. Tait-Bouverie."

"Oh, but they are...."

Betty Neels spent her childhood and youth in Devonshire, England, before training as a nurse and midwife. She was an army nursing sister during the war, married a Dutchman and subsequently lived in Holland for fourteen years. She lives with her husband in Dorset, and has a daughter and a grandson. Her hobbies are reading, animals, old buildings and writing. Betty started to write on retirement from nursing, incited by a lady in the library bemoaning the lack of romance novels.

Don't miss any of our special offers. Write to us at the following address for information on our newest releases.

Harlequin Reader Service
U.S.: 3010 Walden Ave., P.O. Box 1325, Buffalo, NY 14269
Canadian: P.O. Box 609, Fort Erie, Ont. L2A 5X3

BETTY NEELS
Love Can Wait

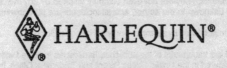

TORONTO • NEW YORK • LONDON
AMSTERDAM • PARIS • SYDNEY • HAMBURG
STOCKHOLM • ATHENS • TOKYO • MILAN • MADRID
PRAGUE • WARSAW • BUDAPEST • AUCKLAND

ISBN 0-373-03636-1

LOVE CAN WAIT

First North American Publication 2001.

Copyright © 1997 by Betty Neels.

All rights reserved. Except for use in any review, the reproduction or
utilization of this work in whole or in part in any form by any electronic,
mechanical or other means, now known or hereafter invented, including
xerography, photocopying and recording, or in any information storage
or retrieval system, is forbidden without the written permission of the
publisher, Harlequin Enterprises Limited, 225 Duncan Mill Road,
Don Mills, Ontario, Canada M3B 3K9.

All characters in this book have no existence outside the imagination of
the author and have no relation whatsoever to anyone bearing the same
name or names. They are not even distantly inspired by any individual
known or unknown to the author, and all incidents are pure invention.

This edition published by arrangement with Harlequin Books S.A.

® and TM are trademarks of the publisher. Trademarks indicated with
® are registered in the United States Patent and Trademark Office, the
Canadian Trade Marks Office and in other countries.

Visit us at www.eHarlequin.com

Printed in U.S.A.

CHAPTER ONE

MR TAIT-BOUVERIE was taking afternoon tea with his aunt—a small, wispy lady living in some elegance in the pleasant house her late husband had left her. She was seventy and in the best of health and, although a kind woman, very taken up with herself and that health. She had long ago decided that she was delicate, which meant that she never exerted herself in any way unless it was to do something she wished to do. She was his mother's older sister, and it was to please his parent that he drove himself down from London to spend an hour with her from time to time.

He was standing at the window overlooking the garden, listening to her gentle, complaining voice cataloguing her various aches and pains, her sleepless nights and lack of appetite—aware that her doctor had recently examined her and found nothing wrong, but nonetheless offering suitable soothing remarks when appropriate.

Someone came into the room and he turned round to see who it was. It was a girl—rather, a young woman—tall, splendidly built and with a lovely face. Her hair, a rich chestnut, was piled tidily on top of her head and she was dressed severely in a white blouse and navy skirt.

She was carrying a tea tray which she set down on the table beside his aunt's chair, arranging it just so without fuss, and as she straightened up she looked at him. It was merely a glance; he was unable to see what colour her eyes were, and she didn't smile.

When she had left the room he strolled over to a chair near his aunt.

'Who was that?' he asked casually.

'My housekeeper. Of course, it is some time since you were last here—Mrs Beckett decided to retire and go and live with her sister, so of course I had to find someone else. You have no idea, James, how difficult it is to get good servants. However, Kate suits me very well. Efficient and rather reserved, and does her work well.'

'Not quite the usual type of housekeeper, surely?'

'She is rather young, I suppose. She had impeccable references—Bishop Lowe and Lady Creswell.'

Mr Tait-Bouverie accepted a cup of tea and handed his aunt the plate of sandwiches. 'Someone local?' he hazarded.

'I believe so. She lives in, of course, but her mother lives locally—a widow, so I am told. Left rather badly off, I hear—which is to my advantage, since Kate needs the job and isn't likely to give her notice. I must say, it is most convenient that she drives a car. I no longer need to hire a taxi to go to Thame to my hairdresser each week—she takes me and does the shopping while I'm at Anton's. It gives her a nice little outing…'

Mr Tait-Bouverie, watching his aunt eating sandwiches with dainty greed, wondered if shopping for food could be regarded as a 'nice little outing'.

'And, of course,' went on Lady Cowder, 'she can cycle to the village or into Thame for anything I need.'

'A paragon,' murmured Mr Tait-Bouverie, and passed the cakestand.

He left half an hour later. There was no sign of the housekeeper as he got into the Bentley. He had half expected her to show him out, but it had been Mrs Pickett, the daily from the village, who had opened the door for him and stood watching him drive away.

Kate watched him too, from the kitchen window. She had to crane her neck to do so, for although she had looked at him in the drawing room it had been a quick glance and she wanted to fill in the gaps, as it were.

Tall, very tall—six and a half feet, she guessed—and a very big man. He had a clever face with a high-bridged nose and a thin mouth, straw-coloured hair going grey and, she supposed, blue eyes. He was a handsome man, she conceded, but there was nothing of the dandy about him. She wondered what he did for a living.

She went back to her pastry-making and allowed a small sigh to escape her. He would be interesting to meet and talk to. 'Not that that is at all likely,' said Kate, addressing the kitchen cat, Horace.

She went presently to clear the tea things away, and Lady Cowder looked up from her book to say, 'The chocolate cake was delicious, Kate. My nephew had two slices. A pity he was unable to stay for dinner.' She gave a titter. 'These men with their girlfriends.'

Kate decided that she wasn't supposed to answer that.

'You asked me to remind you to ring Mrs Johnson, my lady.'

'Oh, yes, of course. It had quite slipped my mind. I have so much to think of.' Lady Cowder closed her book with an impatient frown. 'Get her on the phone for me, Kate.'

Kate put down the tray and picked up the telephone. She still found it difficult to be ordered about without a please or thank you. She supposed it was something she would get used to in time.

Back in the kitchen, she set about preparing dinner. Lady Cowder, despite assuring everybody that she had the appetite of a bird, enjoyed substantial meals. Kate knew now, after almost three months, that her employer's order for 'a morsel of fish and a light sweet' could be interpreted as Dover sole with shrimp sauce, Avergne potato purée, mushrooms with tarragon and a portion of braised celery—followed by a chocolate soufflé or, by way of a change, crème caramel.

It was of no use to allow that to annoy her; she had been lucky to get work so near her home. She suspected that she wasn't being paid quite as much as the going rate for housekeepers, but it included her meals and a small, quite comfortable room. And the money enabled her mother to live without worries as long as they were careful.

Kate had plans for the future: if she could save enough money she would start up on her own, cooking and delivering meals to order. It would need enough capital to buy a van, equipment for the kitchen and money to live on while she built up a clientele. Her mother would help, although for the moment that was out of the question— Mrs Crosby had fallen and broken her arm and, although she made light of it, it was difficult to do much with it in plaster.

When Mrs Crosby expressed impatience about it, Kate sensibly pointed out that they couldn't make plans for a bit—not until she had saved some money. If she could get a hundred pounds she could borrow the rest. It was a paltry sum, but would be an argument in her favour when she tackled their bank manager. It would be a risk but, as she reminded herself constantly, she was twenty-seven and if she didn't take that risk soon it would be too late.

Being a housekeeper was all very well but it was a temporary necessity.

When her father had died suddenly and unexpectedly their world had fallen apart. He had given up his work in a solicitor's office to write a book, the outline of which had already been approved by a well-known publisher. He had given himself six months in which to write it—but within three months, with the research barely completed, he had fallen ill with emphysema and died within six weeks, leaving his wife and daughter with the remnants of the capital that they had been living on.

It had been a risk, a calculated risk which he had been sure was worthwhile, and it was no one's fault. Kate had set about getting their affairs in order and looked around for a job. A sensible girl, she had looked for work which she could do and do well—and when she'd seen Lady Cowder's advertisement for a housekeeper in the local paper she had presented herself to that lady and got the job.

She had no intention of being a housekeeper for a day longer than was necessary; she intended to start a cooked-meals service from her home just as soon as she could save enough money to get it started. But she and her mother had to live—her mother's small pension paid the rent and the running costs of the little house, but they had to eat and keep warm and have clothes. Even with the frugal way in which they lived it would take a couple of years. There were better paid jobs, but they weren't near her home. At least she could go home for her weekly half-day off, and on her day off on Sunday.

It was Sunday the next day—a warm June day with hardly a cloud in the sky, and Kate got onto her bike and pedalled briskly down to the village, thankful to be free for one day. She sighed with content as she pushed her bike up the little path to the cottage where she and her mother lived. It was the middle one of three at the top end of the village main street. It was rather shabby, and the mod cons weren't very 'mod', but the rent was low and the neighbours on either side were elderly and quiet. Not quite what they had been used to, reflected Kate, propping the bike against the back fence and going in through the kitchen door, but it was their home…

Her mother came into the kitchen to meet her. Still a good-looking woman, her russet hair was streaked with grey but her eyes were the same sparkling green as her daughter's.

'You've had a busy morning,' she said with ready sympathy. 'No time for breakfast?'

'I had a cup of tea…'

'You need more than that, a great girl like you,' said her mother cheerfully. 'I'll make a pile of toast and a pot of tea and we'll have lunch early. Come and sit down, love. We'll go into the garden presently.'

Mrs Crosby frowned a little. 'I'm not sure that this job is good for you. Lady Cowder seems a very demanding woman.'

Kate sat down at the kitchen table and Moggerty, their elderly cat, got onto her lap. The room was small but very neat and tidy and the sun shone warmly through the window over the sink. It seemed so much nicer than Lady Cowder's gleaming white tiles and stainless steel. She said mildly, 'It isn't for ever, Mother. Just as soon as we've got a little money saved I'll give it up. And it isn't too bad, you know. I get good food, and my room's quite nice.'

She pulled the breadboard towards her and began to

slice bread for the toast. 'How is your arm? Isn't it next week that you're to have another plaster?'

'Yes, dear. It doesn't hurt at all, and I only wear a sling when I'm out—then no one bumps into me, you see.'

When Kate started to get up her mother said, 'No, dear, I'll make the toast. It's nice to do something for someone other than me, if you see what I mean.'

Her mother was lonely, Kate realised, although she wouldn't admit that. Kate was lonely, too—and though they had a strong affection for each other neither of them were ever going to admit to their loneliness. She said cheerfully, 'We had a visitor yesterday. Lady Cowder's nephew came to tea.'

Mrs Crosby turned the toast. 'Young? Old? What does he do for a living?'

'Youngish—well,' Kate added vaguely, 'In his thirties, I suppose. Very pale hair going grey, and one of those faces which doesn't tell you anything.'

'Good-looking?'

'Yes, but a bit austere. One of those noses you can look down. Enormous and tall.' She began to butter the toast. 'I've no idea what he does. Probably so rich that he does nothing; he was driving a silver-grey Bentley, so he can't be poor.'

'One of those young executive types one is always reading about. Make their million before they're twenty-one, being clever on the stock exchange.'

'Perhaps, but I don't think so. He looked too—too reliable.'

Mrs Crosby regretfully dismissed him as a staid married man. A pity—Kate met so few men. She had had plenty of admirers while her father had been alive but once she and her mother had moved from their comfortable home in the Cotswolds they had gradually dwindled away, much

to Mrs Crosby's regret. Kate hadn't minded in the least—
she had felt nothing but a mild liking for any of them.
She could have married half a dozen times, but for her it
was all or nothing. As she had pointed out to her mother
in her sensible way, if any of the men who had professed
to love her had really done so they would have made it
their business to find out where she and her mother had
gone, and followed them. And done something about it.

Kate, who wanted to marry and have children, could
see that it wasn't very likely that she would get her wish.
Not in the foreseeable future at any rate. She did her best
to ignore her longings and bent all her thoughts on a future which, hopefully, would provide her and her mother
with a livelihood.

Presently they went into the tiny garden behind the cottage and sat under the old plum tree in one corner.

'Once I can start cooking,' said Kate, 'this tree will be
a godsend. Think of all the plums just waiting to be bot-
tled and turned into jam. Perhaps I could specialise in
some kind of plum tart...'

'Not this year,' remarked her mother.

'No, no, of course not. But by the end of next year we
might have enough money to persuade the bank manager.'

Moggerty had gone to sleep on Kate's lap, and presently Kate dozed off too.

She made light of her job, but she was up early and
went to bed late and quite often did the work of two. Lady
Cowder saw no reason to hire more help in the house—
Kate was young and strong, and didn't complain. Besides,
Mrs Pickett came up from the village each morning to
help with the housework. That she was elderly, with ar-
thritis in her knees which didn't allow her to do anything
much below waist level, was something which Lady Cow-

der found unimportant; a hefty young woman like Kate had plenty of energy...

Kate awoke feeling much refreshed, ate a splendid lunch with her mother and later that evening cycled back to Lady Cowder's house, half a mile or so outside the village. She reminded her mother that in three days' time, on her half-day off, they would take the bus into Thame and have a look at the shops. They would take sandwiches and eat them on a bench in the pleasant green gardens around the church, and later treat themselves to tea in one of the teashops.

Taking Lady Cowder's breakfast tray up to her room the next morning, Kate found her sitting up in bed with a pad and pencil. She nodded in reply to Kate's polite good morning, accepted her tray without thanks and said, with more animation than she usually showed, 'My god-daughter is coming to stay—she will arrive tomorrow, so get the guest room overlooking the garden ready. I shall arrange a dinner party for her, of course—Wednesday suits me very well...'

'My half-day off,' Kate reminded her quietly.

'Oh, so it is. Well, you will have to manage without it this week—I'll see that it's made up to you later on. I want Claudia's visit to be a happy one. We can have a few friends in for tennis, tea on the terrace, and perhaps a little supper one evening. Certainly I shall ask friends to come for a drink one evening. We must keep her amused...'

And me run off my feet! thought Kate. She said, without visible annoyance, 'I shall need extra help.'

Lady Cowder looked startled. 'Whatever for? Surely you're capable of a little extra cooking?'

'Of course I am, Lady Cowder, but I can't make beds

and dust and cook meals for dinner parties and suppers, let alone teas. Of course, I could go to the supermarket—they have excellent meals, all ready to warm up.'

Lady Cowder stared at her. Was the girl being impertinent? Seemingly not; Kate had spoken gravely and stood there looking concerned.

'No, no, certainly not. I'll get Mrs Pickett to come for the whole day.'

'She has a niece staying with her,' volunteered Kate, straight-faced. 'I think she is in service somewhere in Oxford—perhaps she would oblige for a few days.'

'Yes, yes, see what you can do, Kate.' Lady Cowder buttered toast and piled on the marmalade. Feeling magnanimous, she added, 'I dare say you can get an hour or so free in the evenings after dinner.'

Kate thought that unlikely. 'I should like to go home for an hour this evening, or perhaps after lunch while you are resting, Lady Cowder. My mother and I had arranged to go out on Wednesday, and I must tell her that I shan't be free.'

'Very well, Kate. As long as it doesn't interfere with your work.' Lady Cowder lay back on her pillows. 'You had better get on. I fancy a light lunch of cold chicken with a salad, and one or two new potatoes. Perhaps one of your jam soufflés to follow. I'll let you know later about dinner.'

Kate went back downstairs, dusted the small sitting room where Lady Cowder sat in the morning, got out the Hoover ready for Mrs Pickett and went to the kitchen to make a pot of tea and butter a plate of scones—Mrs Pickett needed refreshment before she started on her work and so, for that matter, did Kate—although a good deal of her day's work was already done.

Mrs Pickett, sweetened by the tea and scones, agreed to come for the whole day.

'A week, mind, no more than that. Sally will come up for a few hours whenever you need her. She'll be glad of a bit of extra money—the cash that girl spends on clothes... How about a couple of hours in the morning? Nine-ish? Just to make beds and tidy the rooms and clear the breakfast. You'll have your work cut out if Her Nibs is going to have parties and such. Sally could pop in evenings, too—help with laying the table and clearing away. I'll say this for the girl: she's a good worker, and honest.' Mrs Pickett fixed Kate with a beady eye. 'Paid by the hour, mind.'

'How much?'

'Four pounds. And that's cheap. *She* can afford it.' Mrs Pickett jerked her head ceilingwards.

'I'll let you know, and about your extra hours. Would you like to stay for midday dinner and clear up after while I get the cooking started?'

'Suits me. Puts upon you, she does,' said Mrs Pickett. 'Do her good to do a bit of cooking herself once in a while.'

Kate said cheerfully, 'I like cooking—but you do see that I need help if there's to be a lot of entertaining?'

'Lor' bless you, girl, of course I do. Besides, me and the old man, we're wanting to go to Blackpool in September for a week—see the lights and have a bit of fun. The extra cash will come in handy.'

Lady Cowder, informed of all this, shied like a startled horse at the expense. 'Anyone would think that I was made of money,' she moaned. She caught Kate's large green eyes. 'But dear Claudia must be properly entertained, and it is only for one week. Very well, Kate, make whatever arrangements you must. I shall want you here after tea to discuss the meals.'

Mr Tait-Bouverie took off his gloves, stood patiently while a nurse untied his gown, threw it with unerring precision at the container meant for its reception and went out of the theatre. It had been a long list of operations, and the last case hadn't been straightforward so there would be no time for coffee in Sister's office—his private patients would be waiting for him.

Fifteen minutes later he emerged, immaculate and unhurried, refusing with his beautiful manners Sister's offer of coffee, and made his way out of the hospital to his car. The streets were comparatively quiet—it was too late for the evening rush, too early for the theatre and cinemagoers. He got into the Bentley and drove himself home, away from the centre of the city, past the Houses of Parliament, and along Millbank until he reached his home— a narrow house wedged between two imposing town houses, half their size but sharing their view of the river and the opposite bank.

He drove past it to the end of the side street and turned into the mews at the back of the houses, parked the car in the garage behind his house and walked back to let himself in through the front door. He was met in the hall by a short, stout man very correctly dressed in black jacket and pin-striped trousers, with a jovial face and a thick head of grey hair.

His 'Good evening, sir,' was cheerful. 'A splendid summer evening,' he observed. 'I've put the drinks on the patio, sir, seeing as how a breath of fresh air would do you no harm.'

Mr Tait-Bouverie thanked him, picked up his letters from the console table and took himself and his bag off to the study. 'Any messages, Mudd?' he paused to ask, and braced himself as the door at the back of the hall was thrust open and a golden Labrador came to greet him. 'Prince, old fellow, come into the garden—but first I must go to the study…'

'Lady Cowder phoned,' said Mudd. 'Twice. She said she would be glad if you would telephone her as soon as you return home, sir.'

Mr Tait-Bouverie nodded absently and sat down behind his desk in the study, with Prince beside him. There was nothing in the post to take his attention and he went into the sitting room at the back of the house and out onto the small patio facing the narrow walled garden. A drink before dinner, he decided. He would ring his aunt later.

It was a pleasant little garden, with its borders stuffed with flowers and a small plot of grass in its centre. The walls were a faded red brick and covered in climbing roses, veronica and clematis. Mr Tait-Bouverie closed his eyes for a moment and wished he was at his cottage in Bosham—roomy, old and thatched, at the end of Bosham Lane beyond the avenue of oaks and holly trees, within sight and sound of the harbour.

He spent his free weekends there, and brief holidays, taking Mudd and Prince with him, sailing in the creek, working in his rambling garden, going to the pub and meeting friends there… Perhaps he could manage this weekend, or at least Saturday. He had a list next Monday and he had no free time at all until Saturday, but it was only Monday now—he had the whole week in which to arrange things to his satisfaction.

He ate the dinner Mudd set before him and went to his study to phone his aunt.

'James, I was beginning to think you would never tele-

phone. I've tried twice to get you.' She paused, but not
long enough for him to reply.

'Something so exciting. Dear Julia Travers's daughter,
Claudia—my god-daughter, you know—is coming to stay
for a week. Such a dear girl, and so pretty. It's all rather
sudden.' She gave a little laugh. 'But I'm doing my best
to plan a pleasant stay for her. I've arranged a dinner party
for Wednesday evening—just a few friends, and you, of
course. Do say that you can come…eight o'clock. Black
tie.'

Mr Tait-Bouverie listened to this patiently for he was
a patient man. A list of possible excuses ran through his
head but he discarded them. He didn't want to go, but on
the other hand a drive down to Thame in the middle of
the week would make a pleasant break.

'Provided there is no emergency to keep me here, I'll
accept with pleasure,' he told her. 'I may need to leave
directly after dinner, though.'

'Splendid. I'm sure it will be a delightful evening.'

He thought it unlikely. His aunt's friends weren't his,
and the evening would be taken up with time-wasting
chat, but the drive back to London in the evening would
compensate for that.

Lady Cowder talked for another five minutes and he
put down the phone with an air of relief. A few minutes
later he let himself out of his house with Prince and set
off on his evening walk, Wednesday's dinner party already dismissed from his mind. He had several cases for
operation lined up for the week and he wanted to mull
them over at his leisure. Much later he went to his bed to
sleep the sleep of a man whose day had gone well.

Kate, going to her bed, reflected that her day hadn't gone
well at all. After she had given Lady Cowder her lunch

and eaten a hasty snack herself, she'd got into the car and
driven to Thame, where she'd spent an hour or more shopping for the elaborate food decided upon for the dinner
party. When she got home she had been summoned once
more—dear Claudia, she was told, would arrive before
lunch on the following day, so that meal must be something special, and Kate was to make sure that there was
a variety of cakes for tea. Moreover, dinner must be something extra special too.

Unlike Mr Tait-Bouverie's, Kate's day had not gone
well.

Claudia arrived mid-morning, driving her scarlet Mini.
She was small and slender and pretty—a chocolate-box
prettiness—with china-blue eyes, a pert nose, pouting
mouth and an abundance of fair curls. She looked helpless
but Kate, carrying in her luggage, reflected that she
seemed as hard as nails under that smiling face. She had
wasted no time on Kate, but had pushed past her to em-
brace Lady Cowder with little cries of joy which made
Kate feel quite sick.

Kate took the bags up to the guest room, fetched the
coffee tray and retired to the kitchen where Mrs Pickett
was cleaning vegetables.

'Pretty as a picture,' she observed. 'Like a fairy. And
such lovely clothes, too. She won't stay single long, I'll
warrant you.'

Kate said, 'Probably not,' adding silently that Claudia
would stay single just as long as it took her to find a man
with a great deal of money who was prepared to let her
have her own way, and indulge every whim. And if I can
see that in five minutes, she thought, why can't a man?

Her feelings, she decided, mustn't get in the way of her
culinary art. She presented a delicious lunch and forbore

from uttering a word when she handed Claudia the new potato salad and had it thrust back into her hands.

'I couldn't possibly eat those,' cried Claudia. 'Vegetables which have been smothered in some sauce or other; it's a sure sign that they've been poorly cooked and need disguising.'

Lady Cowder, who had taken a large helping, looked taken aback. 'Oh, dear, you don't care for devilled potatoes? Kate, fetch some plain boiled ones for Miss Travers.'

'There aren't any,' said Kate. 'I can boil some, but they will take at least twenty minutes…'

'Well, really… You should have thought of it, Kate.'

'If Miss Travers will give me a list of what she dislikes and likes I can cook accordingly.'

Kate sounded so polite that Lady Cowder hesitated to do more than murmur, 'Perhaps that would be best.'

When Kate had left the room Claudia said, 'What an impertinent young woman. Why don't you dismiss her?'

'My dear, if you knew how difficult it is to get anyone to work for one these days… All the good cooks work in town, where they can earn twice as much. Kate is a good cook, and I must say she runs the house very well. Besides, she lives locally with a widowed mother and needs to stay close to her home.'

Claudia sniggered. 'Oh, well, I suppose she's better than nothing. She looks like a prim old maid.'

Kate, coming in with home-made meringue nests well-filled with strawberries, heard that. It would be nice, she thought, serving the meringues with an impassive face, to put a dead rat in the girl's bed…

Claudia Travers wasn't the easiest of guests. She needed a warm drink when she went to her room at night, a special herb tea upon waking, a variety of yoghurts for breakfast, and coddled eggs and wholemeal bread—all of which Kate provided, receiving no word of thanks for doing so. Claudia, treating her hostess with girlish charm, wasted none of it on Kate.

Lady Cowder took her god-daughter out to lunch the next day, which meant that Kate had the time to start preparing for the dinner party that evening. She was still smarting from her disappointment over her half-day off. No mention had been made of another one in its place, and over breakfast she had heard Claudia observing that she might stay over the weekend—so that would mean no day off on Sunday, either.

Kate, thoroughly put out, started to trim watercress for the soup. There was to be roast duck with sauce Bigarade, and Lady Cowder wanted raspberry sorbets served after the duck. For vegetables she had chosen braised chicory with orange, petits pois and a purée of carrots; furthermore, Kate had been told to make chocolate orange creams, caramel creams and a strawberry cheesecake.

She had more than enough to get on with. The menu was too elaborate, she considered, and there was far too much orange...but her mild suggestion that something else be substituted for the chocolate orange creams had been ignored.

After lunch she started on the cakes for tea. Claudia had refused the chocolate sponge and the small scones Kate had offered on the previous day, so today she made a madeira cake and a jam sponge and, while they were baking, made herself a pot of tea and sat down to drink it.

As soon as Claudia left, she would ask for her day and a half off and go home and do nothing. She enjoyed cooking, but not when everything she cooked was either criticised or rejected. Claudia, she reflected crossly, was a thoroughly nasty young woman.

The cold salmon and salad that she had served for dinner the previous evening had been pecked at, and when Lady Cowder had urged her guest to try and eat something, Claudia had smiled wistfully and said that she had always been very delicate.

Kate had said nothing—but in the kitchen, with no one but the kitchen cat to hear her, she'd allowed her feelings to erupt.

Sally, Mrs Pickett's niece, arrived later in the afternoon. She was a strapping young girl with a cheerful face and, to Kate's relief, a happy disposition. She served tea while Kate got on with her cooking, and then joined her in the kitchen. Mrs Pickett was there too, clearing away bowls and cooking utensils, making endless pots of tea, laying out the tableware and the silver and glass.

Kate, with the duck safely dealt with and dinner almost ready, went to the dining room and found that Sally had set the table very correctly. There was a low bowl of roses at its centre, with candelabra on either side of it, and the silver glass gleamed.

'That's a marvellous job,' said Kate. 'You've made it look splendid. Now, when they have all sat down I'll serve the soup from the sideboard and you take it round. I'll have to go back to the kitchen to see to the duck while you clear the dishes and fetch the hot plates and the vegetables. I'll serve the duck and you hand it round, and we'll both go round with the potatoes and the veg.'

The guests were arriving. Kate poked at her hair, tugged her skirt straight and went to open the door. It was the local doctor and his wife, both of whom greeted her like old friends before crossing the hall to their hostess and Claudia who was a vision in pale blue. Following hard on their heels came Major Keane and his wife, and an elderly couple from Thame who were old friends of Lady Cowder. They brought a young man with them, their nephew. He was good-looking and full of self-confidence. And then, five minutes later, as Kate was crossing the hall with the basket of warm rolls ready for the soup, Mr Tait-Bouverie arrived.

He wished her good evening and smiled at her as she opened the drawing room door. Her own good evening was uttered in a voice devoid of expression.

Mindful of her orders, Kate waited ten minutes then announced dinner and went to stand by the soup tureen. Claudia, she noticed, was seated between the nephew and Mr Tait-Bouverie and was in her element, smiling and fluttering her eyelashes in what Kate considered to be a sickening manner. A pity Sally hadn't spilt the watercress soup down the front of the blue dress, thought Kate waspishly.

Dinner went off very well, and an hour later Kate helped clear the table after taking coffee into the drawing room. Then she went to the kitchen, where the three of them sat down at the kitchen table and polished off the rest of the duck.

'You're tired out; been on your feet all day,' said Mrs Pickett. 'Just you nip outside for a breath of air, Kate. Me and Sally'll fill the dishwasher and tidy up a bit. Go on, now.'

'You don't mind? Ten minutes, then. You've both been such a help—I could never have managed...'

It was lovely out in the garden, still light enough to see around her, and warm from the day's sunshine. Kate wandered round the side of the house and onto the sweep in front of it, and paused to look at the cars parked there: an elderly Daimler—that would be the doctor's—Major

Keane's Rover, a rakish sports car—the nephew's no doubt—and, a little apart, the Bentley.

She went nearer and peered in, and met the eyes of the dog sitting behind the wheel. The window was a little open and he lifted his head and breathed gently over her.

'You poor dear, shut up all by yourself while everyone is inside guzzling themselves ill. I hope your master takes good care of you.'

Mr Tait-Bouverie, coming soft-footed across the grass, stopped to listen.

'He does his best,' he observed mildly. 'He is about to take his dog for a short stroll before returning home.' He looked at Kate's face, pale in the deepening twilight. 'And I promise you, I didn't guzzle. The dinner was superb.'

He opened the door and Prince got out and offered his head for a scratch.

'Thank you,' said Kate haughtily. 'I'm glad you enjoyed it.'

'A most pleasant evening,' said Mr Tait-Bouverie.

Kate heaved a deep breath. 'Probably it was, for you. But this was supposedly my half-day off, and on Sunday, when I should have a full day, I am not to have it because Miss Travers is staying on.' Her voice shook very slightly. 'We—I and my mother—were going to spend the day at Thame, looking at the shops. And my feet ache!'

She turned on her heel and walked away, back to the kitchen, leaving Mr Tait-Bouverie looking thoughtful.

CHAPTER TWO

Mr Tait-Bouverie strolled around the garden while Prince blundered around seeking rabbits, his amusement at Kate's outburst slowly giving way to concern. She had sounded upset—indeed, he suspected that most girls would have given way to floods of tears. Knowing his aunt, he had no doubt that Kate was shown little consideration at the best of times and none at all when Lady Cowder's wishes were likely to be frustrated. He had been touched by her idea of a day's outing to Thame to look at the shops. The ladies of his acquaintance didn't look at shop windows, they went inside and bought whatever they wanted.

He frowned as he remembered that she had said her feet ached...

Back in the house, Claudia fluttered across the room to him. 'Where have you been?' she wanted to know, and gave him a wide smile. 'Are you bored?' She pouted prettily. 'Everyone here, except for Roland, is a bit elderly. 'I'd love to walk in the garden...'

He had beautiful manners and she had no idea how tiresome he found her.

'I'm afraid I must leave, I'm already late for an appointment.'

Claudia looked put out. 'You've got a girlfriend...?'

He answered her in a bland voice which gave no hint

of his irritation. 'No, nothing as romantic, I'm afraid. A patient to check at the hospital.'

'At this time of night? It will be twelve o'clock before you get back to town.'

'Oh, yes. But, you see, people who are ill don't observe conventional hours of sleep.' He smiled down at her pretty, discontented face. 'I must say goodbye to my aunt…'

Lady Cowder drew him a little apart. 'You enjoyed your evening?' she wanted to know. 'Isn't Claudia charming? Such a dear girl and so pretty, is she not?'

'Oh, indeed. A delightful evening, Aunt. The dinner was superb. You have a treasure in your housekeeper, if she did indeed cook it. A big task for her, I should imagine—but doubtless she has ample help.'

'Oh, Kate can do the work of two,' said Lady Cowder airily. 'Of course, I allowed her to have a daily woman to help, and a young girl—she waited at table. Some kind of a niece, I believe. The best we could do at such short notice.'

'You plan more entertainments while Claudia is here?'

'Oh, yes—tennis tomorrow, with tea in the garden and perhaps a buffet supper. And on Friday there will be people coming for drinks, and I dare say several of them will stay on and take pot luck. Claudia thinks she may stay until early next week. I must think up something special for Sunday. A barbecue, perhaps. Kate could manage that easily.'

She would manage, thought Mr Tait-Bouverie, but her feet would be aching fit to kill her by then, and her longed-for day off would be out of the question.

'If Claudia is staying until Monday or Tuesday, why don't you bring her up to town on Friday evening? I'm free for the weekend. We might go to a play on Friday evening, and perhaps go somewhere to dine on Saturday. And she might enjoy a drive down to Henley on Sunday?'

'My dear, James, what a delightful idea. We shall both adore to come. I can leave Kate to look after the house— such a good chance for her to do a little extra work...'

'Oh, you're far too generous for that,' said Mr Tait-Bouverie suavely. 'Let the girl go home for a couple of days; your gardener could keep an eye on the house. I'm sure you will want to reward Kate for such a splendid dinner. Besides, why keep the house open when you can lock up and save on your gas and electricity bills?'

Lady Cowder, who was mean with her money, said thoughtfully, 'You know, James, that *is* a good idea. You have no idea how much this place costs to run and, of course, if I'm not here to keep an eye on Kate she might give way to extravagance.'

'I'll expect you around six o'clock,' said Mr Tait-Bouverie. 'And, if by chance I'm held up, Mudd will take care of you both. You'll come in Claudia's car?'

'Yes. She's a splendid driver. She does everything so well. She will make a splendid wife.'

If she expected an answer to this she was to be disappointed. Her nephew remarked pleasantly that he must leave without delay and embarked on his farewells, saying all the right things and leaving the house by a side door.

He was letting Prince out of the car for a few moments when he heard voices, and saw Mrs Pickett and her niece leaving the house from the kitchen door. They wished him goodnight as they reached him, and then paused as he asked, 'You're going to the village? I'm just leaving, I'll give you a lift.'

'Well, now, that would be a treat for we're that tired, sir.'

'I imagine so.' He opened the car door and they got in carefully.

'You will have to tell me where you live, Mrs Pickett.' He started the car and said over his shoulder, 'What a splendid dinner party. You must have worked very hard.'

'That we did—and that poor Kate, so tired she couldn't eat her supper. Had a busy time of it, with all the shopping and the house to see to as well as concocting all them fancy dishes. Now I hears it's to be a tennis party tomorrow—that means she'll have to be up early, making cakes. Missed her half-day off, too, though she didn't say a word about it.'

Mrs Pickett, a gossip by nature, was in full flood. 'It's not as though she's used to service. She's a lady, born and bred, but she's got no airs or graces, just gets on with it.' She paused for breath. 'It's just along here, sir, the third cottage on the left. And I'm sure Sally and me are that grateful,' she chuckled. 'Don't often get the chance of a ride in such a posh car.'

Mr Tait-Bouverie, brought up to mind his manners by a fierce nanny, got out of the car to assist his passengers to alight—an action which, from Mrs Pickett's view, made her day. As for Sally, she thought she would never forget him.

'I cannot think what possessed me,' Mr Tait-Bouverie told Prince as he drove back to London. 'I have deliberately ruined my weekend in order to allow a girl I hardly know to go and look at shop windows...'

Prince leaned against him and rumbled soothingly, and his master said, 'Oh, it's all very well for you to approve—you liked her, didn't you? Well, I'm sure she is a very worthy person, but I rather regret being so magnanimous.'

* * *

Lady Cowder told Kate the following morning, making it sound as if she was bestowing a gracious favour. She sat up in bed while Kate drew the curtains and put the tea tray beside her.

'There are some employers who would expect their staff to remain at the house during their absence, but, as I am told so often, I am generous to a fault. You may go home as soon as you have made sure that your work is done, and I expect you back on Sunday evening. Harvey, the gardener, will keep an eye on things, but I shall hold you responsible for anything which is amiss.'

'Yes, Lady Cowder,' said Kate, showing what her employer found to be a sorry lack of gratitude. Kate went down to the kitchen to start breakfast for the two ladies, who liked it in bed. More extra work for her.

It would be lovely to have two whole days at home; the pleasure of that got her through another trying day, with unexpected guests for lunch and a great many people coming to play tennis and have tea in the garden.

Mrs Pickett's feet didn't allow her to walk too much, so Kate went to and fro with pots of tea, more sandwiches, more cakes, lemonade and ice cream.

'It's a crying shame,' declared Mrs Pickett, 'expecting you to do everything on your own. Too mean to get help, she is. I suppose she thinks that having Sally last night was more than enough.' Mrs Pickett sniffed. 'It's the likes of her should try doing a bit of cooking and housework for themselves.'

Kate agreed silently.

That evening there was a barbecue, the preparations for which were much hindered by Claudia rearranging everything and then demanding that it should all be returned to its normal place—which meant that by the time the guests began to arrive nothing was quite ready, a circumstance which Claudia, naturally enough, blamed on Kate. With Kate still within earshot, she observed in her rather loud voice, 'Of course, one can't expect the servants to know about these things...'

Kate, stifling an urge to go back and strangle the girl, went to the kitchen to fetch the sausages and steaks.

'Now you can get the charcoal burning,' ordered Claudia.

Kate set the sausages and steaks beside each other on one of the tables.

'I'm wanted in the house,' she said, and whisked herself away.

She made herself a pot of tea in the kitchen, emptied the dishwasher and tidied the room. It was a fine, warm evening, and the party would probably go on for some time, which would give her the chance to press a dress of Claudia's and go upstairs and turn down the beds. First, though, she fed Horace, scrubbed two potatoes and popped them into the Aga for her supper. When they were baked she would top them with cheese and put them under the grill.

One more day, she told herself as she tidied Claudia's room. The drinks party the next day would be child's play after the last few days. She wished Mr Tait-Bouverie joy of his weekend guests, and hoped he was thoughtful of his housekeeper. She wasn't sure if she liked him, but she thought he might be a man who considered his servants...

The barbecue went on for a long time. Kate did her chores, ate her potatoes and much later, when everyone had left and Lady Cowder and Claudia had gone to their rooms, she went to hers, stood half-asleep under the shower and tumbled into bed, to sleep the sleep of a very tired girl.

*   *   *

Since Lady Cowder and her goddaughter were to go to London in the early evening, the drinks party the next day was held just before noon, and because the guests had tended to linger, lunch was a hurried affair. Kate whisked the plates in and out without waste of time, found Lady Cowder's spectacles, her handbag, her pills, and went upstairs twice to make sure that Claudia had packed everything.

'Though I can't think why I should have to pack for myself,' said that young lady pettishly, and snatched a Gucci scarf from Kate's hand without thanking her.

Kate watched them go, heaved an enormous sigh of relief and began to clear lunch away and leave the house tidy. Horace had been fed, and Harvey promised he would be up to see to him and make sure that everything was all right later that evening. He was a nice old man, and Kate gave him cups of tea and plenty of her scones whenever he came up to the house with the vegetables. He would take a look at the house, he assured her, and see to Horace.

'You can go home, Missy,' he told her, 'and have a couple of days to yourself. All that rumpus—makes a heap of work for the likes of us.'

It was lovely to sleep in her own bed again, to wake in the morning and smell the bacon frying for her breakfast and not for someone else's. She went down to the small kitchen intent on finishing the cooking, but her mother wouldn't hear of it.

'You've had a horrid week, love, and it's marvellous to have you home for two whole days. What shall we do?'

'We're going to Thame,' said Kate firmly. 'We'll have a good look at the shops and have tea at that patisserie.'

'It's expensive...'

'We owe ourselves a treat.'

They sat over breakfast while Kate told her mother about her week.

'Wasn't there anyone nice there?' asked Mrs Crosby.

'No, not a soul. Well, there was one—Lady Cowder's nephew. He's very reserved, I should think he has a nasty temper, too. He complimented me on dinner, but that doesn't mean to say that he's nice.'

'But he talked to you?'

'No, only to remark that it had been a pleasant evening.'

'And?'

'I told him that it might have been pleasant for some, and that my feet ached.'

Her mother laughed. 'I wonder what he thought of that?'

'I've no idea, and I really don't care. We'll have a lovely day today.'

A sentiment not echoed by Mr Tait-Bouverie, who had welcomed his guests on Friday evening, much regretting his impulsive action. After suitable greetings he had handed them over to Mudd and, with Prince hard on his heels, had gone to his room to dress. He had got tickets for a popular musical, and Mudd had thought up a special dinner.

Tomorrow, he had reflected, shrugging himself into his jacket, he would escort them to a picture gallery which was all the fashion and then take them to lunch. Dinner and dancing at the Savoy in the evening would take care of Saturday. Then a drive out into the country on Sunday and one of Mudd's superb dinners, and early Monday morning they would drive back.

A waste of a perfectly good weekend, he had thought regretfully, and hoped that Kate was enjoying hers more than he expected to enjoy his. 'Although, the girl is no concern of mine,' he had pointed out to Prince.

Presently he had forgotten about her, listening to Claudia's ceaseless chatter and his aunt's gentle complaining voice. A delicious dinner, she had told him, but such a pity that she wasn't able to appreciate it now that she suffered with those vague pains. 'One so hopes that it isn't cancer,' she had observed with a wistful little laugh.

Mr Tait-Bouverie, having watched her eat a splendid meal with something very like greed, had assured her that that was most unlikely. 'A touch of indigestion?' he had suggested—a remark dismissed with a frown from Lady Cowder. Indigestion was vulgar, something suitable for the lower classes...

He'd sat through the performance at the theatre with every show of interest, while mentally assessing his work ahead for the following week. It would be a busy one— his weekly out-patients' clinic on Monday, and a tricky operation on a small girl with a sarcoma of the hip in the afternoon. Private patients to see, and a trip to Birmingham Children's Hospital later in the week.

In his own world of Paediatrics he was already making a name for himself, content to be doing something he had always wished to do, absorbed in his work and content, too, with his life. He supposed that one day he would marry, if he could find the right girl. His friends were zealous in introducing him to suitable young women in the hope that he would fall in love, and he was well aware that his aunt was dangling Claudia before him in the hope that he would be attracted to her. Certainly she was pretty enough, but he had seen her sulky mouth and suspected that the pretty face concealed a nasty temper.

*   *   *

The weekend went far too quickly for Kate. The delights of window shopping were followed by a peaceful Sunday: church in the morning, a snack lunch in the little garden behind the cottage with her mother and a lazy afternoon. After tea she went into the kitchen and made a cheese soufflé and a salad, and since there were a few strawberries in the garden she made little tartlets and a creamy custard.

They ate their supper together and then it was time for Kate to go back to Lady Cowder's house. That lady hadn't said exactly when she would return—some time early the following morning, she had hinted. Kate suspected that she would arrive unexpectedly, ready to find fault.

The house seemed gloomy and silent, and she was glad to find Horace in the kitchen. She gave him an extra supper and presently he accompanied her up to her room and settled on the end of the bed—something he wouldn't have dared to do when Lady Cowder was there. Kate found his company a comfort, and, after a little while spent listening rather anxiously to the creaks and groans an old house makes at night, she went to sleep—her alarm clock prudently set for half-past six.

It was a beautiful morning; getting up was no hardship. She went down to the kitchen with Horace, fed him generously, let him out and made herself a pot of tea. She didn't sit over it but went back upstairs to dress and then went round the house, opening windows and drawing back curtains while her breakfast egg cooked. She didn't sit over breakfast either—fresh flowers were needed, preparations for the lunch that Lady Cowder would certainly want had to be made, the dining room and the sitting room needed a quick dusting…

Lady Cowder arrived soon after nine o'clock, driven in

a hired car, her eyes everywhere, looking for something she could complain about.

She had little to say to Kate. 'Dear Claudia had to drive to Edinburgh,' she said briefly. 'And my nephew had to leave early, so it seemed pointless for me to stay on on my own. You can cook me a light breakfast; I had no time to have a proper meal before I left. Coddled eggs and some thinly sliced toast—and coffee. In fifteen minutes. I'm going to my room now.'

Lady Cowder wasn't in a good mood, decided Kate, grinding coffee beans. Perhaps the weekend hadn't been a success. Come to think of it, she couldn't believe that she and Claudia and that nephew of hers could have much in common. Although, since he had invited them, perhaps he had fallen in love with Claudia. She hoped not. She knew nothing about him—indeed, she suspected that he might be a difficult man to get to know—but he had been kind, praising her cooking, and he might be rather nice if one ever got to be friends with him.

'And that is most unlikely,' said Kate to Horace, who was hovering discreetly in the hope of a snack. 'I mean, I'm the housekeeper, aren't I? And I expect he's something powerful on the Stock Exchange or something.'

If Mr Tait-Bouverie, immersed in a tricky operation on a very small harelip, could have heard her he would have been amused.

It was some days later, chatting to one of his colleagues at the hospital that he was asked, 'Isn't Lady Cowder an aunt of yours, James? Funny thing, I hear her housekeeper is the daughter of an old friend of mine—he died a year or so ago. Nice girl—pretty too. Fallen on hard times, I hear. Haven't heard from them since they left their place in the Cotswolds—keep meaning to look them up.'

Mr Tait-Bouverie said slowly, 'Yes, I've met her. She seems very efficient, but overworked. My aunt is a kind woman, but incredibly selfish and leaves a good deal to Kate, I believe.'

'I must do something about it.' His elderly companion frowned. 'I'll get Sarah to write and invite them for a weekend.'

'Kate only has Sunday off…'

'Oh, well, they could spend the day. Have they a car?'

'Kate rides a bike.'

'Good Lord, does she? I could drive over and fetch them.'

'Why not invite me, and I'll collect them on my way and take them back on my way home?'

'My dear James, that's very good of you. We'll fix a day—pretty soon, because we're off to Greece for a couple of weeks very shortly and I dare say you've your own holiday planned. 'I'll write to Jean Crosby. They left very quietly, you know; didn't want to make things awkward, if you understand. A bit dodgy, finding yourself more or less penniless. Kate had several young men after her, too. Don't suppose any of them were keen enough, though.'

Mr Tait-Bouverie, overdue for his ward round, dismissed the matter from his mind. He liked Professor Shaw; he was a kindly and clever man, but also absent-minded. He thought it was unlikely that he would remember to act upon his suggestion.

He was wrong. Before the end of the week he was reminded of their plan and asked if he could spare the time for the Sunday after next. 'Sarah has written to Jean and won't take no for an answer, so all you need do is to collect them—come in time for drinks before lunch. Our daughter and her husband will be here, and she and Kate were good friends. Spend the day—Sarah counts on you to stay for supper.'

Mr Tait-Bouverie sighed. It was his own fault, of course—he had suggested driving the Crosbys down. Another spoilt weekend, he reflected, which he could have spent sailing at Bosham.

Kate, arriving home for her day off with barely time to get to church, since Lady Cowder had declared in her faraway voice that she felt faint and mustn't be left, had no time to do more than greet her mother and walk rapidly on to church.

She felt a little guilty at going, for she was decidedly out of charity with her employer. Lady Cowder, cosseted with smelling salts, a nice little drop of brandy and Kate's arm to assist her to the sofa in the drawing room, had been finally forced to allow her to go. She was being fetched, within the hour, to lunch with friends, and when Kate had left she'd been drinking coffee and nibbling at wine biscuits, apparently quite restored to good health.

'This isn't a day off,' muttered Kate crossly, and caught her mother's reproachful eye. She smiled then and said her prayers meekly, adding the rider that she hoped that one day soon something nice would happen.

It was on their way home that her mother told her of their invitation for the following Sunday. 'And someone called Tait-Bouverie is driving us there and bringing us home in the evening...'

Kate came to a halt. 'Mother—that's Lady Cowder's nephew—the one I told about my aching feet.' She frowned. If this was the answer to her prayers, it wasn't quite what she'd had in mind. 'Does he know the Shaws? Professor Shaw's a bit old for a friend...'

'John Shaw and he work at the same hospital; Sarah

said so in her letter. He's a paediatrician—quite a well-known one, it seems.'

'But how on earth did he know about us?'

'John happened to mention our name—wondered how we were getting on.'

'You want to go, Mother?'

'Oh, darling, yes. I liked Sarah, you know, and it would be nice to have a taste of the old life for an hour or two.' Mrs Crosby smiled happily. 'What shall we wear?'

Her mother was happy at the prospect of seeing old friends again. Kate quashed the feeling of reluctance at going and spent the next hour reviewing their wardrobes.

It seemed prudent to tell Lady Cowder that she would want to leave early next Sunday morning for her day off. 'We are spending the day with friends, and perhaps it would be a good idea if I had the key to the side door in case we don't get back until after ten o'clock.'

Lady Cowder cavelled at that. 'I hope you don't intend to stay out all night, Kate. That's something I'd feel bound to forbid.'

Kate didn't allow her feelings to show. 'I am not in the habit of staying out all night, Lady Cowder, but I cannot see any objection to a woman of twenty-seven spending an evening with friends.'

'Well, no. I suppose there is no harm in that. But I expect you back by midnight. Mrs Pickett will have to sleep here; I cannot be left alone.'

Lady Cowder picked up her novel. 'There is a lack of consideration among the young these days,' she observed in her wispy voice. 'I'll have lamb cutlets for lunch, Kate, and I fancy an egg custard to follow. My appetite is so poor...'

All that fuss, thought Kate, breaking eggs into a bowl

with rather too much force, just because I intend to have a whole day off and not come meekly back at ten o'clock sharp.

Lady Cowder, not intentionally unkind, nevertheless delayed Kate's half-day on Wednesday. She had friends for lunch and, since they didn't arrive until almost one o'clock and sat about drinking sherry for another half-hour, it was almost three o'clock by the time Kate was free to get on her bike and go home for the rest of the day.

'I don't know why I put up with it,' she told her mother, and added, 'Well, I do, actually. It's a job, and the best there is at the moment. But not for long—the moment we've got that hundred pounds saved...'

She was up early on Sunday and, despite Lady Cowder's pathetic excuses to keep her, left the house in good time. They were to be called for at ten o'clock, which gave her half an hour in which to change into the pale green jersey dress treasured at the back of her wardrobe for special occasions. This was a special occasion; it was necessary to keep up appearances even if she was someone's housekeeper. Moreover, she wished to impress Mr Tait-Bouverie. She wasn't sure why, but she wanted him to see her as someone other than his aunt's housekeeper.

Presently she went downstairs to join her mother, aware that she had done the best she could with her appearance.

'You look nice, dear,' said her mother. 'You're wasted in that job—you ought to be a model.'

'Mother, dear, models don't have curves and I've plenty—on the ample side, too...'

Her mother smiled. 'You're a woman, love, and you

look like one. I don't know about fashion models, but most men like curves.'

Mr Tait-Bouverie arrived five minutes later, but, judging by the detached glance and his brisk handshake, he was not to be counted amongst that number.

Rather to her surprise, he accepted her mother's offer of coffee and asked civilly if Prince might be allowed to go into the garden.

'Well, of course he can,' declared Mrs Crosby. 'Moggerty, our cat, you know, is asleep on Kate's bed. In any case, your dog doesn't look as though he'd hurt a fly.'

Indeed, Prince was on his best behaviour and, recognising someone who had spoken kindly to him when he had been sitting bored in his master's car, he sidled up to Kate and offered his head. She was one of the few people who knew the exact spot which needed to be scratched.

Kate was glad to do so; it gave her something to do, and for some reason she felt awkward.

Don't be silly, she told herself silently, and engaged Mr Tait-Bouverie in a brisk conversation about the weather. 'It's really splendid, isn't it?' she asked politely.

'Indeed it is. Do you have any plans for your holidays?'

'Holidays?' She blinked. 'No—no. Well, not at present. I'm not sure when it's convenient for Lady Cowder.'

She hoped he wasn't going to talk about her job, and he'd better not try and patronise her...

Mr Tait-Bouverie watched her face and had a very good idea about what she was thinking. A charming face, he reflected, and now that she was away from her job she actually looked like a young girl. That calm manner went with her job, he supposed. She would be magnificent in a temper...

'Did you enjoy your weekend?' he wanted to know,

accepting coffee from Mrs Crosby. 'Cooking must be warm work in this weather.' He gave her a thoughtful look from very blue eyes. 'And so hard on the feet!' he added.

Kate said in a surprised voice, 'Oh, did Lady Cowder tell you that? Yes, thank you.'

She handed him the plate of biscuits and gave one to Prince. 'I dare say he would like a drink before we go.' She addressed no one in particular, and went away with the dog and came back presently with the air of one quite ready to leave.

Mr Tait-Bouverie, chatting with her mother, smiled to himself and suggested smoothly that perhaps they should be going. He settled Mrs Crosby in the front seat, ushered Kate into the back of the car with Prince and, having made sure that everyone was comfortable, drove off.

The countryside looked lovely, and he took the quieter roads away from the motorways. Kate found her ill-humour evaporating; the Bentley was more than comfortable and Prince, lolling beside her, half-asleep, was an undemanding companion. She had no need to talk, but listened with half an ear to her mother and Mr Tait-Bouverie; they seemed to have a great deal to say to each other.

She hoped that her mother wasn't telling him too much about their circumstances. She suspected that he had acquired the art of getting people to talk about themselves. Necessary in his profession, no doubt, and now employed as a way of passing what for him was probably a boring journey.

Mr Tait-Bouverie, on the contrary, wasn't bored. With the skill of long practice, he was extracting information from Mrs Crosby simply because he wished to know more about Kate. She had intrigued him, and while he didn't examine his interest in her he saw no reason why he shouldn't indulge it.

The Shaws gave them a warm welcome, tactfully avoiding awkward questions, and the Shaws' daughter, Lesley, fell easily into the pleasant friendship she and Kate had had.

There was one awkward moment when she remarked, 'I can't think why you aren't married, Kate. Heaven knows, you had all the men fancying you. Did you give them all the cold shoulder?'

It was Mrs Shaw who filled the too long pause while Kate tried to think of a bright answer.

'I dare say Kate's got some lucky man up her sleeve. And talking of lucky men, James, isn't it time you settled down?'

Mr Tait-Bouverie rose to the occasion.

'Yes. It is something I really must deal with when I have the time. There are so many other interests in life...'

There was a good deal of laughter and light-hearted banter, which gave Kate the chance to recover her serenity. For the rest of their visit she managed to avoid saying anything about her job. To the kindly put questions she gave a vague description of their home so that everyone, with the exception of Mr Tait-Bouverie, of course, was left with the impression that they lived in a charming cottage with few cares and were happily settled in the village.

Presumably, thought Mrs Shaw, who had been told about the housekeeper's job, it wasn't quite the normal housekeeper's kind of work. There was talk about tennis parties and a pleasant social life in which, she imagined, Kate took part. Not quite what the dear girl had been accustomed to, but girls worked at the oddest jobs these days.

Mrs Shaw, whose own housekeeper was a hard-bitten

lady of uncertain age who wore print aprons and used no make-up, dismissed Kate's work as a temporary flight of fancy. There was certainly nothing wrong with either Kate's or her mother's clothes...

Mrs Shaw, who didn't buy her dresses at high-street stores, failed to recognise them as such. They were skilfully altered with different buttons, another belt, careful letting-out and taking-in...

Mr Tait-Bouverie did, though. Not that he was an avid follower of women's fashion, but he encountered a wide variety of patients and their mothers—mostly young women wearing just the kind of dress Kate was wearing today. His private patients, accompanied by well-dressed mothers and nannies, were a different matter altogether. He found himself wondering how Kate would look in the beautiful clothes they wore.

He had little to say to her during the day; the talk was largely general, and he took care to be casually friendly and impersonal. He was rewarded by a more open manner towards him; the slight tartness with which she had greeted him that morning had disappeared. He found himself wanting to know her better. He shrugged the thought aside; their encounters were infrequent, and his work gave him little time in which to indulge a passing whim—for that was what it was.

After supper he drove Kate and her mother home. It had been a delightful day and there had been plans to repeat it.

'We mustn't lose touch,' Mrs Shaw had declared. 'Now that we have seen each other again. Next time you must come for the weekend.'

Sitting once more with Prince in the Bentley, Kate thought it unlikely. As it was she was feeling edgy about returning so late in the evening. Even at the speed at which Mr Tait-Bouverie was driving, it would be almost midnight before she got to Lady Cowder's house.

Mr Tait-Bouverie, glancing at his watch, had a very good idea as to what she was thinking. He said over his shoulder, 'Shall I drop you off before I take your mother home? Or do you wish to go there first?'

'Oh, please, it's a bit late—if you wouldn't mind...'

The house was in darkness when they reached it, but that wasn't to say that Lady Cowder wasn't sitting up in bed waiting for her with an eye on the clock.

It was foolish to feel so apprehensive. She worked long hours, and Lady Cowder put upon her quite shamelessly in a wistful fashion which didn't deceive Kate—but she couldn't risk losing her job. She didn't need to save much more before she would be able to see the bank manager...

Mr Tait-Bouverie drew up soundlessly and got out of the car.

'You have a key?'

'Yes. The kitchen door—it's round the side of the house...'

Kate bade her mother a quiet goodnight, rubbed the top of Prince's head and got out of the car.

'Give me the key,' said Mr Tait-Bouverie, and walked silently beside her to the door, unlocked it and handed the key back to her.

'Thank you for taking us to the Shaws',' whispered Kate. 'We had a lovely day...'

'Like old times?' He bent suddenly and kissed her cheek. 'Sleep well, Kate.'

She went past him, closed the door soundlessly and took off her shoes. Creeping like a mouse through the house, she wondered why on earth he had kissed her. It had been a careless kiss, no doubt, but it hadn't been necessary...

CHAPTER THREE

KATE found herself thinking about Mr Tait-Bouverie rather more than she would have wished during the next day or so. Really, she told herself, there was no reason for her to do so. They were hardly likely to meet again, and if they did it wouldn't be at a mutual friend's house. She told herself that his kiss had annoyed her—a careless reward, a kind of tip. Her cheeks grew hot at the very idea. She dismissed him from her mind with some difficulty—but he stayed there, rather like a sore tooth, to be avoided at all costs.

Lady Cowder was being difficult. She seldom raised her voice but her perpetual, faintly complaining remarks, uttered in a martyr-like way, were difficult to put up with. She implied, in the gentle voice which Kate found so hard to bear, that Kate could work a little harder.

'A big strong girl like you,' she observed one lunchtime, 'with all day in which to keep the place in good order. I don't ask much from you, Kate, but I should have thought that an easy task such as turning out the drawing room could be done in an hour or so. And the attics—I am sure that there are a great many things there which the village jumble sale will be only too glad to have. If I had the strength I would do it myself, but you know quite well that I am delicate.'

Kate, offering a generous portion of sirloin steak with its accompanying mushrooms, grilled tomatoes, French-fried onions and buttered courgettes, murmured meaninglessly. It was a constant wonder to her that her employer ate so heartily while at the same time deploring her lack of appetite.

Because she needed to keep her job, she somehow contrived to arrange her busy days so that she could spend an hour or so in the attics. There was a good deal of rubbish there, and a quantity of old clothes and pots which no self-respecting jumble sale would even consider, but she picked them over carefully in the hope of finding something worth offering. It was a thankless task, though, and took up any spare time she had in the afternoons. So it was that when Mr Tait-Bouverie called she knew nothing of his visit until he had gone again.

'Really,' said Lady Cowder in her gentle, complaining voice, 'it was most inconvenient, Kate. You were up in the attics and there was no one to get us tea...'

'I left the tea tray ready, Lady Cowder.'

'Yes, yes, I know that, but poor James had to boil the kettle and make the tea himself. As you know, I have had a headache all day and did not dare to leave the chaise longue.'

The idea of 'poor James' having to make his own tea pleased Kate. Serve him right, she reflected waspishly. And there had been only thinly cut bread and butter and sponge cake for tea, since Lady Cowder had declared that her digestion would tolerate nothing richer. He would have gone back home hungry.

Kate didn't bother to analyse her unkind thoughts—which was a pity for he had gone to some trouble to do her a good turn.

Mr Tait-Bouverie had gone to see his aunt on a request from his mother, and he hadn't wanted to go. His leisure hours were few, and to waste some of them on a duty visit went against the grain—although he'd had to admit that the prospect of seeing Kate again made the visit more tolerable.

Lady Cowder had been pleased to see him, regaling him in a plaintive little voice with her ill-health, deploring the fact that Kate had taken herself off to the attics so that there was no one to bring in the tea tray.

Mr Tait-Bouverie had made the tea, eaten a slice of the cake Kate had left on the kitchen table while he boiled the kettle and borne the tray back to the drawing room. He was a kind man, despite his somewhat austere manner, and he had listened patiently while his aunt chatted in her wispy voice. Presently he had striven to cheer her up.

'I'm going to Norway in a week or so,' he told her. 'I am to give some lectures in several towns there, as well as do some work in the hospitals. I was there a few years ago and they asked me to go back. It's a delightful country…'

'Ah, you young people with your opportunities to enjoy yourselves around the world—how fortunate you are.'

He agreed mildly. There wouldn't be much opportunity to enjoy himself, he reflected—the odd free day, perhaps, but certainly not the social life he felt sure his aunt envisaged. Not being a very sociable man, except with close friends, he hardly thought he would miss that.

His aunt ate the rest of the bread and butter in a die-away fashion, while at the same time deploring her lack of appetite.

'Perhaps a holiday would improve my health,' she observed. 'I have never been to Norway but, of course, I couldn't consider it without a companion.'

Mr Tait-Bouverie, a man who thought before he spoke, for once allowed himself to break this rule.

'Then why not go? Surely a companion won't be too hard to find?'

'The cost, dear boy...'

He remained silent; Lady Cowder could afford a dozen companions if she wished, but, as his mother had told him charitably, 'Your aunt has always been careful of her money.'

Lady Cowder glanced at the empty cakestand. 'Really, I don't know what I pay Kate for—my wants are so simple, and yet she seems unable to offer me even a simple meal.'

Mr Tait-Bouverie wished that Kate would come down from the attics; he had no more than a passing interest in her but she intrigued him. He said, half jokingly, 'Why should you pay for a companion? Take Kate with you. She seems to be a woman of good sense, capable of smoothing your path...'

Lady Cowder sat up straight. 'My dear James, what a splendid idea. And, of course, I need only pay her her usual wages. She will be delighted to have the opportunity to travel. Tell me, where would you recommend that we should stay?'

Mr Tait-Bouverie hadn't expected his suggestion to be taken so seriously. 'Kate might not wish to go to Norway...' he said. 'Though at this time of year one of the smaller villages around the fiords would be delightful. Very quiet, of course, but by no means cut off from civilisation—these places attract many visitors in the summer months. Or you could stay in Bergen—a pleasant small city with everything one could wish for.'

'Could you arrange it for me?'

'I'm so sorry, Aunt. I'm not free to do that. My trip to Norway has been arranged, of course. I suggest that you get hold of a good travel agent and get him to see to everything. That is, if you intend to go.'

'Of course I intend to, James. I'll tell Kate in the morning and she can see to the details.'

'She might not wish to go.'

'Nonsense. It's the chance of a lifetime for the girl. A free holiday and nothing to do. I hardly think it necessary to pay her her wages at all—after all, she won't need to spend any money.'

Mr Tait-Bouverie lifted an eyebrow. 'I don't think that would be legal. You wouldn't wish to be involved in a court case.'

'Certainly not. She will, of course, have to make herself useful.'

'If she agrees to go with you...'

'She can have a month's notice if she refuses,' said Lady Cowder tartly.

Mr Tait-Bouverie, his duty visit paid, took himself off home. There had been no sign of Kate, and the thought crossed his mind that he might have done her a disservice. He reminded himself that she was a young woman capable of managing her own affairs. She had only to refuse to go and look for another job.

He dismissed the whole affair from his mind but, all the same, it returned to bother him during the next few days.

Kate, bidden to the drawing room by one of the old-fashioned bells which still hung in the kitchen, took off her apron, tucked an errant russet tress behind an ear, and went upstairs. The sack? she wondered. Or, far worse, another visit from Claudia. She opened the door, went into the room and stood quietly, waiting to hear whatever news her employer had for her.

Lady Cowder stared at her. Really, the girl didn't look like a housekeeper and certainly didn't behave like one; she didn't even look interested...

'I have decided to take a holiday, Kate. I need relaxation. My palpitations must be a sign of something more serious although, as you know, I am never one to worry about myself. I intend to go abroad—to Norway. You will come with me. I need someone to take care of me, see to travel arrangements and so on. It is a pleasant surprise to you, no doubt, to have a holiday which will cost you nothing. I shall, of course, continue to pay you your wages. You may consider yourself very fortunate, Kate.'

Kate said quietly, 'Are you asking me to go away with you, Lady Cowder?'

'Well, of course—have you not been listening?'

'Yes, but you haven't asked me if I wish to go, Lady Cowder.'

Lady Cowder turned a shocked gaze upon her. 'You are my housekeeper, Kate. I expect you to do what I wish.'

'If I am asked,' said Kate calmly. 'And I would prefer not to go, Lady Cowder. I am sure you will have no difficulty in finding a suitable companion.'

'And you expect to remain here, being paid for doing nothing?'

Kate didn't answer, and Lady Cowder spent a few moments in reflection. She didn't want to give Kate the sack—she was hard-working, a splendid cook and hadn't haggled over her wages. Nor was she a clock-watcher, everlastingly going on about her rights. To engage a companion, even for a month, would cost money—something Lady Cowder couldn't contemplate without shuddering...

There was only one solution. She said, in the wispy voice she used when she wanted sympathy, 'Please consider my offer, Kate. It would be for a month, and I am prepared to pay you the normal wages of a companion—considerably more than you get at present. Of course, when we return your wages will revert to the present amount.'

'What exactly would my wages be, Lady Cowder?' asked Kate pleasantly.

Lady Cowder closed her eyes and assumed a pained expression. She was thinking rapidly. Mrs Arbuthnott, a friend of hers, had just engaged a new companion and her salary seemed excessive, although Lady Cowder had been assured that it was the standard rate. Surely half that amount would be sufficient for Kate; that would still be almost twice as much as her present money.

Lady Cowder opened her eyes and told Kate.

Twice as much, thought Kate, and if she could save all of it she would soon have the money she needed. She said quietly, 'Very well, Lady Cowder, I will come with you. When do you intend to go?'

'As soon as possible, while I still have my health and strength. Go to Thame tomorrow morning and see the travel agents. I wish to fly—first class, of course—and stay at one of the smaller towns situated close to the fiords. A good hotel, not isolated, with all the amenities I am accustomed to.'

'You want me to bring back particulars of several places so that you may choose?'

'Yes, yes. And some possible dates—within the next two weeks.' Lady Cowder sank back against the cushions. 'Now bring me my coffee. I could eat a biscuit or two with it.'

Kate, watching the coffee percolate, weighed the doubtful delights of travelling with her employer against twice as much money for a month. She didn't expect to enjoy herself, but it would mean that she would be able to give up this job sooner than she had expected. It would also mean careful budgeting; her mother would have to manage on her pension while Kate was away so that every spare penny of her wages could be saved.

'The chance of a lifetime,' Kate told Horace, offering him a saucer of his favourite cat food. 'I shall become a famous cook and live happily ever after.'

She told her mother when she went home for her half-day.

'Darling, what a stroke of luck...' Mrs Crosby got a pencil and the back of an envelope and began to do sums. The result was satisfactory and she nodded and smiled. Then she frowned. 'Clothes—a hotel—you'll need clothes...'

'No, I shan't, Mother. There's that mole-coloured crêpe thing I had years ago. That'll do very well if I have to change for the evening. Lady Cowder wouldn't expect me to be fashionable, and no one will know us there.' She thought for a moment. 'There is also that black velvet skirt—if I borrow your silk blouse, that'll do as well. I'll only need skirts and blouses and sweaters during the day, and the navy jacket and dress will do to travel in.'

'One or two summer dresses?' suggested Mrs Crosby. 'It's July, love, it could be very warm.'

'I'll take a couple of cotton dresses. But I'm a bit vague about the weather there—for all I know it might even be getting cooler! I should have asked at the travel agents, but there was so much to discuss. I'm to drive us to Heathrow and leave the car there, and the flight should be easy enough. We're to be met by a taxi at the airport and taken to the hotel in Bergen that Lady Cowder has chosen. She wants to spend a day or two there before we go to Olden;

there's a modern hotel there. It's a small village on the edge of a fiord. I do wonder if Lady Cowder is going to like it. A whole month...'

'Let's hope she will get to know some of the people staying there. She plays bridge, doesn't she? Hopefully so will they; that will give you some free time. I can't think why she can't go alone. She's elderly, but she's quite fit, and there would be plenty of help at the kind of hotels she stays at.'

'I'd much rather have been left to caretake—but don't forget all the extra money, Mother. And a month goes quickly enough.'

'Money isn't everything,' observed Mrs Crosby.

'No, but it does help...it *is* a stroke of luck.'

Something she had to remind herself of during the next ten days, for Lady Cowder's orders and counter-orders were continuous. Her entire wardrobe had to be inspected, pressed, packed—and then unpacked, because she had changed her mind as to what she would or would not take. Kate's patience was sorely tried.

The ten days went quickly and Kate, busy from early morning until late at night, had little time to think her own thoughts. All the same, from time to time she thought about Mr Tait-Bouverie. She had to admit to herself that she would have liked to know more about him. 'Not that he would remember me,' she said to herself as she re-packed Lady Cowder's cases for the third time.

Mr Tait-Bouverie hadn't forgotten her. The thought of her wove through his head like a bright ribbon, disrupting his erudite ponderings over the lectures he was to give at the various hospitals to which he had been invited in Norway. Only by an effort was he able to dismiss her from his mind as he stepped onto a platform and embarked on the very latest advances in paediatrics. It would not do, he told himself firmly; the girl was disrupting his work as well as his leisure hours. He even dreamed of her...

Surprisingly, the journey to Bergen went smoothly. Kate drove to Heathrow, deaf to Lady Cowder's back-seat driving while she went over in her mind all the things she had to see about in order to get them safely to the hotel in Bergen. She guided her employer safely onto the plane, assured her for the tenth time that the car had been safely parked, that she had the tickets in her handbag, that the plane was perfectly safe and that they would be met at the airport in Norway.

Lady Cowder assumed the air of an invalid once on board, and asked wistfully for a glass of brandy—as she felt faint. She murmured, 'My heart, you know,' when the stewardess brought it to her, and she smiled bravely at the two passengers on the other side of the gangway. She then sank back with her eyes closed, and stayed that way until they were airborne and lunch was served.

'Perhaps you would prefer just a little soup?' suggested the stewardess.

'How kind,' murmured Lady Cowder. 'But I believe that a small meal might give me the strength I shall need when we land.'

Kate listened to all of this nonsense with some amusement, tinged with dismay. A month of this and it would be she who would be the invalid, not Lady Cowder.

Lady Cowder was helped off the plane with great care, Kate following burdened with scarves, handbags and books. Once they were alone, Lady Cowder said sharply, 'Well, don't just stand there, Kate—find whoever it is who is to meet us.'

This was easily done, seeing that he was standing with a placard in his hand with Lady Cowder's name on it. A pleasant man, he went with Kate to collect their luggage, settled Lady Cowder in the back of the car and held the door open for Kate.

'Get in front, Kate,' said Lady Cowder. 'I need to be quiet for a time. I'm exhausted.'

Kate did as she was told, thinking thoughts best left unsaid, then cheered up in response to the driver's friendliness.

There was so much to see as he drove; her spirits rose as he pointed out anything which he thought might interest her and by the time they reached Bergen, she was ready to enjoy every minute of their stay there. He indicated the fish market, the shops, and the funicular to the top of the mountain behind the town, then asked how long they would be staying.

'Only two days. I don't suppose I'll have time to see everything, but I'll do my best.'

An optimistic remark, as it turned out.

The Hotel Norje, in the centre of the town, was everything anyone could wish for—even Lady Cowder gave her opinion that it was comfortable. She had a splendid room overlooking the Ole Nulle Plass—a handsome square opening into a park—and an equally splendid bathroom.

'You may unpack at once,' she told Kate, 'and phone for tea. You had better have a cup before you go to your room. I shall rest for an hour or so and dine later.'

Kate poured tea for both of them, unpacked Lady Cowder's luggage and disposed of it in cupboards and drawers, only too aware that in a couple of days she would have to pack it all again. She did it silently and competently, then went down to Reception to collect her room key.

Her room was on the floor above Lady Cowder's. It was nicely furnished, but lacked the flowers, bowl of fruit and comfortable chairs. There was no bathroom either; a small shower cubicle was curtained off in one corner. Kate unpacked what she would need for a day or so, showered, got into the mole crêpe and went back to her employer.

'Go and get your dinner. You can tidy the room while I'm in the restaurant, and wait here. I shall probably need some help with getting to bed; I'm utterly exhausted.'

Kate, her tongue clenched between her splendid teeth, went down to the restaurant. Obviously Lady Cowder didn't intend to eat with her housekeeper.

Not that Kate minded—she was hungry, and ate everything set before her—soup, cod, beautifully cooked, and a dessert of cloud berries and cream. She sat over her coffee, oblivious of the admiring glances cast at her. Despite the sombre dress, her lovely face and magnificent person made a striking picture. Indeed, several people wished her good evening as she left the restaurant, and she answered them with her serene smile.

She paused at the reception desk to ask about sending letters to England, accepted a free postcard, wrote on it then and there and left it for the receptionist to post, with the promise of paying for the stamp in the morning. She would have liked to have phoned her mother, but she had only a small amount of English money. She would have to go to a bank in the morning and change some of it.

Lady Cowder greeted her crossly. 'What a very long time you have been, Kate. Had you forgotten that I was waiting for your return until I could go to dinner?'

Kate, mellowed by good food and the friendly glances she had received, said cheerfully, 'You could have come down to the restaurant, Lady Cowder—there was no need to wait for me.'

Quite the wrong answer. 'See that someone brings me a warm drink when I return, and tidy the room and bathroom. I sent the chambermaid away. I can't find my travelling clock; you had better look for it.'

Kate found the clock, tidied the bathroom and sat down in one of the easy chairs to wait. She was going to earn every penny of that extra money, she reflected, but it would be worth it. She spent some time thinking about her plans for the future, and then allowed her thoughts to dwell on Mr Tait-Bouverie. She was sorry for him, having an aunt as disagreeable as Lady Cowder. She wondered if his mother was like her. Perhaps that was why he wasn't married. To have a mother like that was bad enough, to be married to a woman of the same nature would be disastrous.

Her musings were cut short by Lady Cowder's return. She declared that she must go to bed immediately—which didn't prevent her from wanting this, that and the other before Kate was at last told that she might go.

In her room at last, Kate took a quick shower and got into bed. Her last thought was one of thankfulness that Lady Cowder was going to have her breakfast in bed and didn't wish to be disturbed until ten o'clock. A splendid chance to nip out directly after she had had breakfast and take a quick look at the town.

Kate woke early and got up at once. It was a grey morning, but that didn't deter her from her plan. She went downstairs and found several other people breakfasting. They greeted her pleasantly and waved her towards the enormous centre-table loaded with dishes of herrings, cheese, bacon, eggs and sausages. It seemed that one helped oneself and ate all one wanted. She piled her plate, asked for coffee, and sat down at a table by herself, only to be invited to join a group of young men and women close by. They were on holiday, they told her, on their way to the north of the country. When she told them that she knew nothing of Norway, they told her where to go and what to see.

'You are alone?' they asked.

'No. I'm travelling with an elderly lady—I'm her housekeeper in England.'

'So you are not free?'

'No. Only for an hour or two when it is convenient for her.'

'Then you must not lose time. The shops will be open soon, but the fish market is already busy. Go quickly and look there; it is a splendid sight.'

It was an easy walk down the main shopping street, and well worth a visit. It wasn't just the fish, although they were both colourful and splendid, it was the flower stalls, bulging with flowers every colour of the rainbow. Kate went from one to the other and longed to buy the great bunches of roses and carnations, thinking how delightful it would be to buy a whole salmon and take it back home. Impossible, of course. She caught sight of a clock and hurried back in time to present herself in Lady Cowder's room.

There was no reply to her civil good morning.

'Go down to the desk and arrange for a car to drive us out to Troldhaugen—Edward Grieg, the composer, lived there—we will return here for lunch. Make sure that the driver is a steady man.'

Kate, not sure how she was to do that, decided to ignore it and hope for the best. Their driver turned out to be a youngish man who spoke excellent English and was full of information. Kate listened to every word, but Lady Cowder closed her eyes and asked Kate to give her the smelling salts.

They had to walk a short distance to the house, something which they hadn't known about. Lady Cowder, in unsuitable shoes, declared that the walk would tire her, but rather grudgingly agreed to Kate having a quick look.

There were other tourists there with their guides, but Kate, given a strict ten minutes, didn't dare linger.

All the same, when she returned to the car, she was expected to give an account of what she had seen. Kate suspected that when they returned to England and Lady Cowder met her friends again she would wish to recount her activities in Norway. A little knowledge of Grieg's house and Kate's impressions of it would be useful in conversation...

Kate didn't escape for the rest of that day. Lady Cowder had little desire to stroll around looking at the shops; certainly the fish market had no attraction. She intended to take the funicular to the top of Mount Floyen.

'It would, of course, be much nicer to go by car, but that would take time and probably not be worth the journey. Besides, I'm told everyone goes by the funicular.'

Kate held her tongue, afraid that if she ventured an opinion they might not go at all.

It was raining when Kate got up the next morning. It rained a great deal in Bergen, the friendly receptionist told her, but that didn't deter her from putting on her raincoat and tying a scarf over her head and hurrying out as soon as she had breakfasted. This was their last day in Bergen, and the chances were that Lady Cowder would refuse to go out at all.

The funicular was out of the question, so were the various museums. If she walked very fast she could get a glimpse of the Bryggen, with its medieval workshops and old buildings. She started off down the main street towards Torget and the Bryggen, head down against the rain, only to be brought to a sudden halt against a vast Burberry-covered chest.

'Good morning, Kate,' said Mr Tait-Bouverie. 'Out early, aren't you?'

She goggled up at him, rain dripping from her sodden scarf.

'Well, I never...!' She gulped and added sedately, 'Good morning, sir.'

Since he made no move to go on his way, she added politely, 'You don't mind if I go on? I haven't much time.'

He gripped her arm gently. 'To do what, Kate?'

'Well, Lady Cowder doesn't like to be disturbed until ten o'clock, so I want to see as much as I can before then.' She added hopefully, 'I expect you're busy.'

'Not until midday. Where are you going?'

She told him, trying not to sound impatient.

'In that case—' he lifted a hand at a passing taxi '—allow me to make up for the delay I have caused you.'

He had bundled her neatly into the taxi before she could draw breath.

'It is a little after half-past eight; you have more than an hour. Tell me, how long have you and my aunt been here?'

'We're here for two days; we go to Olden later today— for three weeks.'

'I shall be surprised if my aunt remains there for so long. It is a delightful little place, but, beyond the hotel, there isn't much to do. There are ferries, of course, going to various other small villages around the fiords, but I doubt if she would enjoy that.' The taxi stopped. 'Here we are, let us not waste time.'

For all the world as though I didn't want to see the place, thought Kate crossly, getting out of the taxi and ignoring his hand.

She said coldly, 'Thank you for the taxi, Mr Tait-Bouverie. I'm sure you have other plans...'

He took her arm. 'None at all, Kate.' He led her down a wide passage lined with old wooden houses. 'Let us have a cup of coffee and you can recover your good humour.'

'I have only just had breakfast,' said Kate, still coldly polite. A remark which was wasted on him. The wooden houses, so beautifully preserved, housed small offices, workshops and a couple of cafés. She found herself sitting in one of them, meekly drinking the delicious brew set before her.

'They make very good coffee,' observed Mr Tait-Bouverie chattily.

'Yes,' said Kate. 'It's very kind of you to bring me here, but really there is no need...'

A waste of breath. 'Your mother is well?' he asked.

'Yes, thank you. The plaster is to come off very shortly.' Kate finished her coffee and picked up her gloves. 'I'd better be getting on. Thank you for the coffee, sir.'

Mr Tait-Bouverie said pleasantly, 'If you call me "sir" just once more, Kate, I shall strangle you!'

She gaped at him. 'But of course I must call you "sir," Mr Tait-Bouverie. You forget that I'm in your aunt's employ—her housekeeper.'

'There are housekeepers and housekeepers, and well you know it. You may cook divinely, dust and sweep and so on with an expert hand, but you are no more a housekeeper than I am. I am not by nature in the habit of poking my nose into other people's business—but it is obvious to me, Kate, that you are housekeeping for a reason. Oh, I'm sure you need the money in order to live, but over and above that I confess that I am curious.'

Kate said coolly, 'I'm sure that my plans are of no interest to you, s—Mr Tait-Bouverie.'

'Oh, but they are. You see, I can think of no reason why you should work for my aunt. I dare say she underpays you, certainly she works you hard. She may be my aunt, but I should point out that my visits to her are purely in order to reassure my mother, who is her younger sister and feels that she must keep in touch.'

'Oh, have you a mother?' Kate went pink; it was a silly question, deserving a snub.

'Indeed, yes.' He smiled faintly. 'Like everyone else.'

He lifted a finger and asked for more coffee and, when it had been brought, settled back in his chair. 'Are you saving for your bottom drawer?' he asked.

'Heavens, no. Girls don't have bottom drawers nowadays.'

'Ah—I stand corrected. Then why?'

It was obvious she wasn't going to escape until she had answered him. 'I want to start a catering business. Just from home—making simple meals to order, cooking for weddings and parties—that sort of thing.'

'Of course. You are a splendid cook and manager. Why don't you get going?'

It was a relief to tell someone about her schemes. For a moment she hesitated at telling this man whom she hardly knew and would probably not meet again on equal terms. But she felt reckless. Perhaps it was being in foreign places, perhaps it was the caffeine in all the coffee she was drinking.

'I'm saving up,' she told him. 'You see, if I can go to the bank and tell the manager that I've a hundred pounds he might lend me the money I need.'

Mr Tait-Bouverie looked placid, although he doubted very much if a bank manager would see eye to eye with Kate. A hundred pounds was a very small sum these days: it might buy dinner for two at a fashionable restaurant in London, or two seats for the latest play; it might be enough to pay the electricity bill or for a TV licence, but one could hardly regard it as capital.

He said in a kind voice, 'Do you have much more to save?'

'No. That's why I've come with Lady Cowder. She has said she will double my wages if I act as her companion while she is here.'

He nodded. 'I have often wondered, what do companions do?'

'Well, they are just there—I mean, ready to find things and mend and iron—and talk, if they're asked to. And buy tickets and see about luggage and all that kind of thing.'

'Will you get any time to yourself?' He put the question gently and she answered readily.

'I'm not sure—but I don't think so. I mean, not a day off in the week or anything like that.'

'In that case, we have just fifteen minutes to take a quick look around while we're here. There's a rather nice shop along here that does wood carvings and some charming little figures—trolls. Have you bought a troll to take home?'

She shook her head. 'Not yet...'

He bought her one, saying lightly, 'Just to bring you luck.'

They went back to the hotel by taxi presently, and when

it stopped, Kate asked, 'Are you coming in? Shall I tell Lady Cowder you're here?'

He said unhurriedly, 'No, I must go to the hospital very shortly and later today I'm going to Oslo. No need to say that we met, since there is no chance of my aunt seeing me.'

Kate offered a hand. 'Thank you for taking me to the Bryggen and giving me coffee. Please forget everything I told you. I shouldn't have said anything, but I don't have much chance to talk to anyone. Anyway, it doesn't matter, does it? We don't meet—I mean, like this.'

He smiled down at her lovely face, damp from the rain. All he said was, 'I do hope you enjoy your stay in Norway.'

She didn't want to go into the hotel; she would have liked to have spent the day with him. The thought astonished her.

CHAPTER FOUR

LADY Cowder was sitting up in bed eating a good breakfast.

'They tell me it is raining,' she informed Kate. 'There seems no point in staying here. Go down to the desk and arrange for a car to take us to Olden. I wish to leave within the next two hours.'

It was a complicated journey—Kate had taken the trouble to read the various leaflets at the reception desk—involving several ferries, and quite a distance to go. But there would be no need to get out of the car, she was assured, unless they wished to stop for refreshment on the way. It would be prudent, decided Kate, to get the clerk to phone the hotel at Olden. She asked for the bill, asked if coffee could be sent up to Lady Cowder's room in an hour's time, and went back upstairs. There was all the packing to see to...

The rain stopped after they had been travelling for an hour, and by the time they reached Gudvangen there was blue sky and sunshine.

'Tell the driver to take us to a hotel for lunch,' said Lady Cowder.

He took them up a hair-raisingly steep road. 'Nineteen hairpin bends,' he told them proudly, 'and a gradient of one in five. A splendid view is to be had from the top.'

'But the hotel?' queried Lady Cowder faintly. She had

been sitting with her eyes closed, trying not to see the sheer drop on either side of the road.

'A splendid hotel,' promised the driver. As indeed it was. Once inside, with her back to the towering mountains and the fiord far below, Lady Cowder did ample justice to the smoked salmon salad she was offered. The driver had taken it for granted that he would have his lunch with his passengers, so he and Kate carried on an interesting conversation while they ate.

Olden, it seemed, was very small, although the hotel was modern and very comfortable. 'There are splendid walks,' said the driver, looking doubtfully at Lady Cower. 'There are also shops—two or three—selling everything.'

Lady Cowder looked so doubtful in her turn that Kate hastily asked to be told more about the hotel.

Presently they took the ferry, after another hair-raising descent to the village below, and crossed the Sognefjord to Balestrand to rejoin the road to Olden. Quite a long journey—but not nearly long enough for Kate, craning her neck to see as much as possible of the great grey mountains crowding down to the fiord. She was enchanted to see that wherever there was a patch of land, however small, squashed between the towering grey peaks, there were houses—even one house on its own. Charming wooden houses with bright red roofs and painted walls.

'Isn't it a bit lonely in the winter?' she asked.

The driver shrugged. 'It is their life. The houses are comfortable, there is electricity everywhere, they have their boats.'

Olden, when they reached it, was indeed small—a handful of houses, a small landing stage and, a little way from the village, the hotel. Reassuringly large and modern, its car park was half-full. Lady Cowder, who had had little to say but had somehow conveyed her disapproval of the scenery, brightened at the sight of it.

Certainly their welcome lacked nothing in warmth and courtesy. She was led to her room, overlooking the fiord, and assured that a tray of tea would be sent up immediately, together with the dinner menu.

Kate unpacked, went down to the reception desk to make sure that their driver had been suitably fed and went to find him. He had been paid, of course, but Lady Cowder had added no tip, nor her thanks. Kate handed him what she hoped was sufficient and added her thanks, knowing that Lady Cowder would want an account of everything Kate had spent from the money she had been given for their expenses. She would probably have to repay it from her own wages but she didn't care—the man had been friendly; besides, he had told her that he had five children.

Her room, she discovered, was two floors above Lady Cowder's and at the back of the hotel, its windows looking out towards the mountains. It was obviously the kind of room reserved for such as herself: companions, Ladies' maids, poor relations. It was comfortable enough but it had no shower, and the bathroom was at the end of the passage to be shared with several other residents. She didn't mind, she told herself—and felt humiliation deep down.

She was to eat her dinner early and then return to Lady Cowder's room and wait for her there, occupying herself with the odd jobs: buttons to sew on, odds and ends to find, things to be put ready for the night.

She enjoyed dinner; the dining room was elegant and the food good. The brown crêpe hardly did justice to her surroundings, but she forgot that in the satisfaction of discovering that there were several English people staying at

the hotel. Moreover, they looked to be the kind of people
Lady Cowder might strike up a passing acquaintance with.
Kate, straining her ears to catch their conversation, was
delighted to hear that they were discussing bridge, a game
her employer enjoyed.

She finished her coffee and went back to Lady
Cowder's room, and listened with outward serenity to that
lady's grumbles about a crumpled dress. Alone, she tidied
up, fulfilled the odd jobs she had been given to do, arranged for Lady Cowder's breakfast to be brought to her
in her room and then went to look out of the window.

The sky had cleared and the last of the evening sun was
lighting the sombre mountains, making the snow caps that
most of them wore glisten. But if the mountains were
sombre, there was plenty of life going on beneath them.
Passengers were going aboard a ferry, and she wished that
she was going with them to some other small village,
probably isolated except for the ferries which called there.
Not that she sensed any loneliness amongst the people she
had met so far—indeed, they seemed happy and perfectly
content.

Who wouldn't be, she reflected, living in such glorious
surroundings? As far as she could discover, communica-
tions were more than adequate; the driver had told her
more in a couple of hours than any guide book could have
done. She watched the ferry until it was out of sight round
a distant bend in the fiord, and then she drew the curtains—Lady Cowder's orders.

Her employer was in a good temper when she returned.
'So fortunate,' she observed. 'There are several English
people staying here, only too glad to make up a table for
bridge. They tell me that this hotel is most comfortable;
I am glad I decided to come here.'

* * *

After the first few days Kate agreed with her. A bridge table was set up each afternoon and she was free for several hours to do as she liked. She spent the first afternoon walking to the village, which was cheerfully full with visitors, its one shop bustling with tourists. It sold everything, she discovered, not only souvenirs but clothes and shoes, household goods and food. She bought cards to send home, walked to the end of the village and then retraced her steps, stopping to admire the smart men's outfitters displaying the latest male fashions—wondering when they would be worn in such a small community.

A ferry had just come in, and she spent some time watching the cars landing and the passengers coming ashore. There were plenty of people waiting to board, too, and she wanted very much to know where it was going. In a day or two, she promised herself, when she felt more at home in her surroundings, she would find out.

After that afternoon she got bolder. She went a little further each day, stopping to ask the way, discovering that English seemed to come as easily to the Norwegians as their own tongue. Greatly daring, she took the bus to Loen, a pretty village some kilometres away from Olden. She had no time to explore it, for Lady Cowder had told her that she must be in the hotel by five o'clock, ready to carry out her wishes, but at least, she told herself, she had been there.

She had suggested that Lady Cowder might like to hire a car and visit some of the neighbouring villages herself, only to be told that it wasn't for her to suggest what they should do.

'I should have thought,' said Lady Cowder, sounding reproachful, 'that you were more than grateful for the splendid time that you are having. Heaven knows, there is little enough for you to do.'

It wasn't a companion that Lady Cowder needed, thought Kate. A lady's maid would have been nearer the mark. Kate, who had a kind heart, felt sorry for her employer, being so incapable of doing the simplest thing for herself. Perhaps she had had a husband who'd spoilt her and seen to it that she never had to worry about anything.

'Very nice, too,' said Kate, addressing a handful of sheep peering at her from their pasture, which was sandwiched between two frowning mountains. 'But who on earth is likely to wrap me in carefree luxury?'

She walked on past the sheep, and along a narrow road running beside the fiord. She wished her mother could have been with her. Never mind the mundane tasks she was given to do, the indifference of her employer, the small—perhaps unintentional—pinpricks meant to put her in her place a dozen times a day; she was happy to be in this peaceful land. Just as long as the bridge parties continued each afternoon, life would be more than tolerable.

It was the following morning, when she went as usual to find out what Lady Cowder wanted her to do before she went down to breakfast, that she found that lady in a bad temper. She ignored Kate's good morning, and told her to pull the curtains and fetch her a glass of water.

'The Butlers are leaving today.' She spoke with the air of a martyr. 'There is no one else in this place who is willing to make up a table for bridge. I shall die of boredom.' She looked at Kate as though it was her fault.

'Perhaps there will be some other guests...'

'I have enquired about that—something you might have done if you had been here. There are no English or Americans expected. I intend to leave here. There is a good hotel at Alesund; the Butlers have stayed there and recommend it. Go downstairs to the reception desk and tell them that we are leaving tomorrow. Then phone the hotel and get rooms.'

She handed Kate a slip of paper with the name of the hotel and the phone number on it. 'I require a comfortable room; I hardly need remind you of that. Get a room for yourself. Those with a shower are cheaper, and it doesn't matter if it isn't on the same floor as mine. Now hurry along and do as I ask instead of standing there, saying nothing.'

Kate went down to talk to the clerk at the reception desk. Why had they come all this way? she wondered. Lady Cowder could have played bridge just as easily at home. She set about the business of smoothing Lady Cowder's progress through Norway.

Alesund was a large town, built on several islands, and the hotel was, fortunately, to Lady Cowder's liking. It had all the trappings she found so necessary for her comfort— a uniformed porter at its door, bell boys to see to the luggage, a smiling chambermaid and willing room-service. Her room, the lady was pleased to admit, was extremely comfortable—and there was a number of Americans and English staying at the hotel.

Kate unpacked once again, listened to a list of instructions without really hearing them, and went to find her own room, which was two flights up with a view of surrounding rooftops. It was comfortable, though, and she had her own shower. She hung up her few clothes and went down to make sure that Reception knew about Lady Cowder's wishes. She found some information leaflets, too, and took them back with her to read later.

Hopefully they would stay here for the rest of their time in Norway—they had been only nine days at Olden; there were still more than two weeks before they returned to England. Kate prayed that there would be an unending flow of bridge players for the next few weeks. Certainly, there were several Americans in the foyer.

She went back to Lady Cowder to tell her this, and was told to order tea to be sent up.

'And you can get yourself tea, if you wish,' said Lady Cowder, amiable at the prospect of suitable company.

Mr Tait-Bouverie, finding himself with several days of freedom between lectures, reminded himself that his aunt might be glad to see him. It was his duty, he told himself, to keep an eye on her so that he could assure his mother that her sister was well. At the same time he could make sure that Kate was having as good a time as possible.

It annoyed him that he was unable to forget her while at the same time remaining unwillingly aware of her. He reminded himself that his interest in her was merely to see if she would achieve her ambition and branch out on her own. She was a competent girl, probably she would build up a solid business cooking pies and whatever.

He drove himself to Olden, to be told at the hotel there that Lady Cowder had given up her room and gone to Alesund. So after lunch he drove on, enjoying the grand scenery, queueing for the ferries as he came to them, going unhurriedly so that he had the leisure to look around him. He had been on that road some years earlier, but the scenery never failed to delight him.

It was four o'clock by the time he reached the hotel at Alesund and its foyer was nearly full. He saw Kate at once, standing with her back to him, reading a poster on a wall. He crossed to her without haste, tapped her lightly on the shoulder and said, 'Hello, Kate.' He was aware of a deep content at the sight of her.

Kate had turned round at his touch and for a moment her delight at seeing him again was plain to see. Though only for a moment. She wished him good afternoon in a quiet voice from a serene face. She asked at once, 'Have you come to see Lady Cowder? I'm sure she will be delighted to see you...'

'Are you delighted to see me?'

She prudently ignored this. 'She plays bridge until five o'clock every afternoon.' She glanced at her watch. 'I'm just waiting here until she's ready for me.'

'Your free time?' He wanted to know.

'Yes, every afternoon unless there's something...' She paused. 'I've seen quite a lot of the town,' she added chattily. 'Walking, you know, one can see so much more...'

He had a mental picture of her making her lonely way from one street to the next with no one to talk to and no money to spend. He put a hand under her elbow and said gently, 'Shall we sit down and share a pot of tea? If you'll wait here while I get a room and order tea...'

He sat her down in a quiet corner of the lounge alongside the foyer and went away, to return within minutes followed by a waitress with the tea tray, a plate of sandwiches and a cakestand of tempting cream cakes.

'Be mother,' said Mr Tait-Bouverie. Kate, he could see, was being wary, not sure of herself, so he assumed the manner in which he treated his childish patients—an easy-going friendliness combined with a matter-of-fact manner which never failed to put them at their ease.

He watched Kate relax, passed the sandwiches and asked presently, 'Do you suppose my aunt intends to stay here for the rest of her holiday?'

'Well, as long as there are enough people to make up a four for bridge. I think she is enjoying herself; it's a very comfortable hotel and the food is excellent, and so is the service.'

'Good; I shall be able to send a satisfactory report to my mother. What happens in the evenings?'

He watched her select a cake with serious concentration.

'I believe there's dancing on some evenings. I—I don't really know. I dine early, you see, and then go and wait for Lady Cowder to come to bed.'

'Surely my aunt is capable of undressing herself?' He frowned. 'And why do you dine early? Don't you take your meals together?'

Kate went pink. 'No, Mr Tait-Bouverie. You forget—I'm your aunt's housekeeper.' She saw the look on his face and added hastily, 'I don't take my meals with Lady Cowder in her own home.'

'That is entirely another matter. So you don't dance in the evenings?'

She shook her head. 'I'm having a lovely holiday,' she told him earnestly.

A statement of doubtful truth, reflected Mr Tait-Bouverie.

It was two minutes to five o'clock. 'I must go,' said Kate. 'Thank you for my tea.' She hesitated. 'I dare say you would like to surprise Lady Cowder?'

'No, no. I'll come up with you. Is she in her room?'

'There is a card room on the first floor. I go there first...'

She sounded so unenthusiastic at the thought of his company that Mr Tait-Bouverie found himself smiling, then wondered why.

It had struck five o'clock by the time they reached the card room. Lady Cowder was sitting with her back to the door, but she heard Kate come in. Without turning round, she said, in the rather die-away voice calculated to win sympathy from her companions, 'You're late, Kate, and I have such a headache. I dare say you forgot the time.' She glanced at her three companions. 'It is so hard to get a really reliable...' She paused, because they were all looking towards the door.

Mr Tait-Bouverie, a large hand in the small of Kate's back propelling her forward, spoke before Kate could utter.

'Blame me, Aunt. I saw Kate as I arrived and kept her talking. I was surprised to find that you had left Olden, and she explained—'

'My dear boy,' said Lady Cowder in a quite different voice. 'How delightful to see you. Have you come all this way just to see how I was enjoying myself? I hope you can stay for a few days.'

She got up and offered a cheek for his kiss, then turned to the three ladies at the bridge table. 'You must forgive me. This is my nephew; he's over here lecturing and has come to see me.'

He shook hands and made all the usual polite remarks, aware that Kate had returned to stand by the door, watching, ignored. She might have been a piece of furniture.

'We shall see you this evening?' asked one of the ladies.

'Certainly. We shall be dining later.' He turned to his aunt. 'At what time do you and Kate have dinner, Aunt?'

Lady Cowder looked uncomfortable. 'I dine at half past eight, James.' She smiled brightly at her bridge companions. 'I'm sure we shall all meet presently.'

She said her goodbyes and went to the door. Mr Tait-Bouverie, following her, slipped a hand under Kate's elbow and smiled down at her.

The three ladies were intrigued; his Aunt was outraged. Alone with him presently she said, 'You forget, James, Kate is my housekeeper.'

He agreed placidly. 'Indeed I do; anyone less like a housekeeper I have yet to meet.'

'And it is quite impossible to dine with her...'

Mr Tait-Bouverie's blue eyes were hard. 'Can she not manage her knife and fork?' he enquired gently.

'Yes, of course she can. Don't be absurd, James. But she hasn't the right clothes.'

'Ah,' said Mr Tait-Bouverie, and added reflectively, 'You and my mother are so different, I find it hard to remember that you are sisters.'

Lady Cowder preened herself. 'Well, we aren't at all alike. I was always considered the beauty, you know, and your mother never much cared for a social life. It has often surprised me that she should have married your father. Such a handsome and famous man.'

'My mother married my father because she loved him and he loved her. I see no surprise in that.'

Lady Cowder gave a little trill of laughter. 'Dear boy, you sound just like your father. Isn't it high time you married yourself?'

'I think that perhaps it is,' said Mr Tait-Bouverie, and wandered away to his own room.

Kate, summoned presently to zip up a dress, find the right handbag and make sure that Reception hadn't forgotten Lady Cowder's late-night hot drink, was treated to unusual loquacity on the part of her employer.

'My nephew has plans to marry,' she observed, already, in her mind's eye, seeing Claudia walking down the aisle smothered in white tulle and satin. 'He is, of course, a most eligible man, but dear Claudia is exactly what he needs—pretty and well dressed, and used to his way of life. The dear girl must be in seventh heaven.'

She surveyed her reflection in the pier-glass, nodded in

satisfaction and glanced briefly at Kate. Not really worth a glance in that brown...

Mr Tait-Bouverie, dining presently with his aunt, behaved towards her with his usual courtesy, but refused to be drawn when she attempted to find out if he had plans to marry soon.

As they drank their coffee he asked idly, 'Where is Kate? Off duty?'

'Waiting for me in my room. I'm sure she is glad to have an hour or so to herself.' Lady Cowder added virtuously, 'I never keep her up late.'

They went presently to the small ballroom where several couples were dancing to a three-piece band. When he had settled his aunt with several of her acquaintances, James excused himself.

'But it's early, James,' his aunt protested. 'Do you care to dance for a while? I'm sure there are enough pretty girls...'

He smiled at her. 'I'm going to ask Kate to dance with me,' he told her.

Kate, leaning out of the window to watch the street below, withdrew her head and shoulders smartly at the knock on the door. Lady Cowder occasionally sent for her, wanting something or other, so Kate called, 'Come in,' and went to the door to meet the messenger.

Mr Tait-Bouverie came in quietly and shut the door behind him. 'If you could bear with a middle-aged partner, shall we go dancing?'

Kate stopped herself just in time from saying yes. Instead she said sedately, 'That's very kind of you to ask me, sir, but I stay here in the evenings in case Lady Cowder should need me.'

'She doesn't need you; she is with people she knows. I have told her that we are going to dance.'

'And she said that I could?'

Mr Tait-Bouverie, a man of truth, dallied with it now. 'I didn't hear her reply, but I can't see that she can have any objection.'

Kate had allowed common sense to take over. 'Well, I can. I mean, it just won't do.' And then, speaking her thoughts out loud, she added, 'You're not middle-aged.'

'Oh, good. You consider thirty-five still youthful enough to circle the dance floor?'

'Well, of course. What nonsense you talk…' She stopped and started again. 'What I should have said…'

'Don't waste time trying to be a housekeeper, Kate.'

He whisked her down to the ballroom at a tremendous pace and danced her onto the floor.

It had been some years since Kate had gone dancing, but she was good at it. It took only a few moments for her to realise that Mr Tait-Bouverie was good at it, too. Oblivious of Lady Cowder's staring eyes, the glances from the other guests, the brown dress, she allowed herself to forget everything save the pleasure of dancing with the perfect partner—for despite his vast size he was certainly that. He didn't talk, either, for which she was thankful. Just dancing was enough…

The music stopped and she came down to earth. 'Thank you, sir, that was very nice. Now, if you will excuse me…'

'Kate, Kate, will you stop being a housekeeper for at least this evening? You aren't *my* housekeeper, you know. The band's starting up again—good. And did I ever tell you that I shall wring your neck if you call me "sir"? I should hate to do that, for you are a magnificent dancer— big girls always are.'

Kate drew a deep breath. 'How very rude,' she told him coldly. 'I know I'm large, but you didn't have to say so...'

'Ah, the real Kate at last. Did I say big? I should have said superbly built, with all the curves in the right places, and a splendid head of hair.'

Kate had gone very pink. 'I know you're joking, but please don't. It—it isn't kind...'

'I don't mean to be kind. You see, Kate, I want to see behind that serene face of yours and discover the real Kate. And I'm not joking, only trying to get to know you—and it seems to me that the only way to do that is to stir you up.'

The music stopped once more and he took her arm. 'Let us take a walk.'

'A walk? Now? But in an hour Lady Cowder will go to bed.'

'We can walk miles in an hour. Go and get a jacket or shawl or something while I tell her.'

Kate gathered her wits together. 'No, no. Really, I can't! I'd love to, but I really mustn't.'

For answer he took her arm and trotted her across the room to where his aunt sat.

'I'm taking Kate for a brisk walk,' he told her. 'I'm sure you won't mind, Aunt. It's a pleasant evening and we shan't be gone long. Do you need Kate again before you go to bed?'

'Yes—no...' Lady Cowder was bereft of words for once. 'I dare say I can manage.'

'I'll knock when I come in, Lady Cowder,' said Kate in her housekeeper's voice. 'But if you would prefer me not to go, then I'll not do so.'

Lady Cowder looked around her at several interested faces.

'No, no, there's no need. Go and enjoy yourself.' She added wistfully, 'How delightful it must be to be young and have so much energy.' She smiled around her, and was gratified by the approving glances. She was, she told herself, a kind and considerate employer, and Kate was a very fortunate young woman. Poor James must be feeling very bored, but he was always a man to be kind to those less fortunate than himself.

They walked the short distance to the harbour, which thrust deep into the centre of the town, and walked around it. It was still light and quite warm, and there were plenty of people still about. Mr Tait-Bouverie sauntered along beside Kate, talking of this and that in a pleasantly casual manner, slipping in a question here and there so skilfully that she hardly noticed what a lot she was telling him.

On their way back to the hotel he observed, 'Since I'm here with a car I'll drive you to the nearest two islands tomorrow. You're free in the afternoon?'

Kate said cautiously, 'Well, I am usually—but if Lady Cowder wants to go anywhere or needs me for something...'

'Like what?'

'Well—something; I don't know what.'

He said softly, 'You don't need to make excuses if you don't want to come with me, Kate.'

She stopped and looked up at him. 'Oh, but I do, really I do. You have no idea...'

She paused, and he finished for her. 'How lonely you are...?'

She nodded. 'I feel very ungrateful, for really I have nothing much to do and I don't suppose I'll ever have the chance to come here again.'

'But you are lonely?'

'Yes.'

He began to tell her about the islands. 'Unique,' he told her. 'Connected by tunnels under the sea, and the islands themselves are charming. There is a small, very old church with beautiful murals; we'll go and look at it.'

At the hotel she wished him goodnight. 'It was a lovely evening,' she told him. 'Thank you.'

He stared down at her upturned face. He knew as he watched her smile that he was going to marry her. He could see that there would be obstacles in his path, not least of which would be Kate's wariness as to his intentions once he declared them. But he had no intention of doing that for the moment. First he must get behind that calm façade she had adopted as his aunt's housekeeper and find the real Kate. He was a patient man and a determined one; he had no doubt as to the outcome, but it might take a little time.

He said with cheerful friendliness, 'Goodnight, Kate. I'll see you tomorrow around two o'clock.'

Kate paused on her way to her room, wondering if she should knock on Lady Cowder's door—and then decided not to. She had said that there was no need, hadn't she? Besides, Kate hated the idea of the cross examination to which she would be subjected.

She stood under the shower for a long time, remembering her delightful evening. It was strange how Mr Tait-Bouverie seemed to have changed. He was really rather nice. She got into bed and lay thinking about tomorrow's trip. She would have a lot to write home about, she thought sleepily.

She was on the point of sleep when she remembered that Mr Tait-Bouverie was going to marry Claudia. If she hadn't been half-asleep already the thought would have upset her.

*   *   *

Lady Cowder wasn't in a good mood in the morning. Kate
was sent away to press a dress which should have been
done yesterday. 'But, of course, if you aren't here to do
your work, what can one expect?' asked Lady Cowder,
adopting her aggrieved, put-upon voice. Kate said nothing, seeing her chances of being free in the afternoon
dwindling. She was aware that her employer disapproved
of her nephew having anything to do with her, and would
interfere if she could.

Kate had reckoned without Mr Tait-Bouverie, who took
his aunt out for a drive that morning, gave her coffee at
a charming little restaurant and drove to the top of Mount
Aksla so that she might enjoy the view over Alesund.

'You're playing bridge this afternoon?' he wanted to
know. 'Supposing I take Kate for a short drive? I want to
visit a rather lovely old church, and she might as well
come with me.' He added cunningly, 'It is very good of
you to allow her to have the afternoons free. She seems
to have explored the town very thoroughly.'

Lady Cowder smiled complacently. 'Yes, she may do
as she likes between two and five o'clock each day and,
heaven knows, I am the easiest mistress any servant could
wish for. Take her with you by all means; this holiday
must be an education to her.'

Mr Tait-Bouverie swallowed a laugh. His aunt had had
a sketchy education—governesses, a year in Switzerland—
and had never made any attempt to improve upon it.
Whereas he knew from what Kate's mother had told him
during one of his seemingly casual conversations, that Kate
had several A levels and would have gone on to a univer-
sity if her father hadn't wanted her at home to help research
his book.

'Just so,' he said mildly, and drove his aunt back to the hotel.

Kate, brushing and hanging away Lady Cowder's many clothes, was quite startled when that lady came into her room.

'I have had a delightful morning,' she announced. 'And I have a treat in store for you, Kate. Mr Tait-Bouverie has offered to take you for a drive this afternoon. I must say it is most kind of him, and I hope you will be suitably grateful both to him and to me. Now go and have your lunch and come back here in case I need anything before I go to lunch myself.'

Kate skipped down to the restaurant, gobbled her food and hurried to her room. She wondered what Mr Tait-Bouverie had said to make Lady Cowder so amenable. Perhaps she could ask him; on the other hand, perhaps not. He was making a generous gesture and probably wasn't looking forward to the whole afternoon in her company. What on earth would they talk about for three hours?

She got into the jersey dress she hadn't yet worn. It was by no means new, but it fitted her and the colour was a warm mushroom—it toned down her bright hair nicely. Her shoulderbag and shoes had seen better days, too, but they were good leather and she had taken care of them. She went downstairs, wondering if Mr Tait-Bouverie had left a message for her at the desk. She had told him that she was usually free soon after two o'clock, but now that she saw the time she saw that she was much too early. It would never do to look too eager. She turned round and started back up the stairs.

'Cold feet, Kate?' asked Mr Tait-Bouverie, appearing

beside her, apparently through the floor. 'I'm ready if you are.'

She paused in mid-flight. 'Oh, well, yes. I'm quite ready, only I'm too early.'

'I've been waiting for the last ten minutes,' he told her placidly. 'It's a splendid day; let us cram as much into it as we can.'

Kate was willing enough. She was led outside to where his hired Volvo stood, ushered into it, and, without more ado, they set off.

'Giske first,' said Mr Tait-Bouverie, driving away from the town and presently entering a tunnel. 'I hope you don't mind the dark? This goes on for some time—more than a couple of miles—but it is used very frequently, as you can see, and is well maintained. Giske is rather a charming island—it's called the Saga island, too. We'll go and see that church, and then drive over to Godoy and have tea at Alnes. It's quite a small village but there's a ferry, of course, and in the summer there are tourists...'

His placid voice, uttering commonplace information, put her quite at her ease. She wasn't sure if she liked the tunnel very much—driving through the mountain with all that grey rock and presently, as he pointed out to her, under the fiord—but he was right about Giske. It was peaceful and green, even with the mountains towering all round it. There were few cars, the sun shone and the air was clear and fresh.

Kate took a deep breath and said, 'This is nice.'

The little church delighted her, so very small and so perfect, with ancient murals on its walls and high-backed pews. It was quiet and peaceful, too; she could imagine that the peace went back hundreds of years. Mr Tait-Bouverie didn't say much but wandered round with her, and when she had had her fill he took her outside to the little churchyard with its gravestones bright with flowers.

'It's something I'll remember,' said Kate, getting back into the car.

They drove on to Godoy then, through small villages, their houses beautifully kept. And when they reached Alnes they had tea at the small hotel opposite the ferry. By now Kate had forgotten to be wary and become completely at ease.

Mr Tait-Bouverie watched her lovely face and was well content, taking care not to dispel that.

CHAPTER FIVE

KATE, making a splendid tea, was happy to have someone
to talk to, to answer her questions, who was apparently
as happy as she was. After a couple of weeks of no conversation—for Lady Cowder only gave orders or made
observations—it was delightful to say what she thought
without having to make sure that it was suitable first, and,
strangely enough, she found that she could talk to Mr
Tait-Bouverie.

'We should be going,' he told her presently. 'A pity,
for it is such a pleasant day.' He smiled at her across the
table. 'There's another very long tunnel ahead.'

'Longer than the other one?'

'Yes. But there's plenty of time; we are quite near to
Alesund.'

'It's been a lovely afternoon,' said Kate, getting into
the car, wishing the day would never end. In a little over
an hour she would be getting into the brown crêpe dress,
ready to eat her solitary dinner. She frowned, despising
herself for allowing self-pity to spoil the day. Besides,
there was still the drive back...

The tunnel took her by surprise; one moment they were
tooling along a narrow road edged with thick shrubs, giving way to trees as they climbed the mountain beyond,
the next they were driving smoothly between grey rock.
True, the tunnel was lighted, and there was a stream of
traffic speeding past them, but, all the same, she caught

herself wondering how many minutes it would be before they came out into daylight again.

Mr Tait-Bouverie said soothingly, 'It takes less than five minutes, although it seems longer.' He added, 'You don't like it very much, do you? I should have asked you about that before we left the hotel. There are any number of other places to visit.'

'No, oh, no, I've loved every minute—and really, now we are in the tunnel, I truly don't mind. I wouldn't like to drive through it alone, though.'

He laughed. 'You're honest, Kate. Even if you don't exactly enjoy it, it's something you will remember.' He glanced at the dashboard. 'We're exactly halfway.'

The sudden sickening noise ahead of them seemed to reverberate over and over again through the tunnel—a grinding, long drawn-out noise accompanied by shouts and screams. And the lights went out.

Mr Tait-Bouverie brought the car to a smooth halt inches from the car ahead of him as other cars passed him, unable to slow their pace quickly enough, colliding inevitably. He could have said the obvious; instead he observed calmly, 'A pity about the lights,' and reached for the phone beside his seat.

Kate, who hadn't uttered a sound, said now in a voice which shook only very slightly, 'I expect someone will come quickly,' and thought what a silly remark that was. 'Were you phoning for help? You were speaking Norwegian?'

'Yes, and yes. Now, Kate, perhaps we can make ourselves useful. I'm sure everyone with a phone has warned Alesund, but the more helpers there are the better. Come along!'

He reached behind him and took his bag from the back seat. 'How lucky that I've my bag with me. I don't care to leave it at the hotel. Stay where you are; I'll come round and open your door, then follow me and do as I say. You're not squeamish, are you?'

It didn't look as though she would be given the chance to be that. She said meekly, 'I don't think so.'

'Good; come along, then.'

They didn't have far to go—a van had gone out of control and slewed sideways so that the car behind it had crashed into it, turned over and been pushed by another car against the wall, presumably with such force that the lighting cables had been damaged.

There were a great many people milling around, some of them already hauling people from damaged cars. Mr Tait-Bouverie, holding Kate fast by the hand, spoke to a man kneeling beside a woman whose leg was trapped under the wheel of a car.

'I'm a doctor; can I help?'

He had spoken in Norwegian and the man answered him in the same language, shining his torch on Mr Tait-Bouverie and then on Kate. 'English, aren't you? God knows how many there are trapped and hurt. I've told people to go back to their cars. There is a nurse somewhere, and several men giving a hand.' He glanced at Kate again. 'The young lady?'

'Not a nurse, but capable. She will do anything she is asked to do.'

'Good. Can she help the nurse? Over there with those two children? This young woman—if you could look at her? Tell us what to do—most of us have some knowledge of first aid....'

'Off you go,' said Mr Tait-Bouverie to Kate. 'I'll find you later.'

I must remember, thought Kate rather wildly, picking

her way towards the nurse, to tell him that he is a rude and arrogant man.

Then she didn't think about him again; there was too much to do.

The nurse, thank heavens, spoke excellent English. Kate tied slings, bandaged cuts and held broken arms and legs while the nurse applied splints made of umbrellas, walking sticks and some useful lengths of wood someone had in their boot.

She was aware of Mr Tait-Bouverie from time to time, going to and fro and once coming to kneel beside her to find and tie a severed artery. The nurse had told her to apply pressure with her fingers while she fetched the doctor and Kate knelt, feeling sick as blood oozed out despite her efforts. Mr Tait-Bouverie didn't speak until he had controlled the bleeding. 'Bandage it tightly with anything you can find.'

He had gone again. Kate, feeling queasy, took the clean handkerchief she saw in the patient's pocket and did the best she could.

It seemed like hours before she heard the first sounds of help arriving. It had only been minutes—minutes she never wished to live through again. Even though help was on the way it took time to manoeuvre the cars out of the way so that the ambulances and the fire engines could get through. Everyone was quiet now, doing as they were told, backing out of the tunnel whenever it was possible, making more room.

She was suddenly aware that there was a man crouching beside the old lady she was trying to make comfortable.

'You are a nurse?' he asked in English.

'No. Just helping. I'm with a doctor—a surgeon, actually. Mr Tait-Bouverie.'

'Old James? Splendid. He's around?' He didn't wait for an answer, but began to question the old lady. He looked up presently. 'Concussion and a broken arm. She's worried about her handbag. She was thrown out of her car...'

'Which car? I'll look for it.'

It was an elderly Volvo, its door twisted, its bodywork ruined. Kate climbed in gingerly and it creaked under her weight. The bag was on the floor, its contents spilled. She collected everything she could see and began to edge out backwards.

'There you are,' said Mr Tait-Bouverie. He sounded amused. 'Even if you are back to front, I'm glad to see that you're none the worse for all this.'

He stopped and lifted her neatly the right way up, out of the car.

Kate said coldly, 'Thank you, Mr Tait-Bouverie. There was no need of your help.'

'No, I know, but the temptation was too strong.' He looked her over. 'You look rather the worse for wear.'

She started back to the old lady. 'Well, I am the worse for wear,' she told him tartly, and thought vexedly that he looked quite undisturbed—his jacket over his arm, his shirt-sleeves rolled up. His tie was gone—used for something or other, she supposed. He still looked elegant.

Kate, conscious that her hair was coming down, her hands were filthy and scratched and her dress stained and torn, turned her back on him.

He was there, beside her, exchanging greetings with the Norwegian doctor while she handed over the handbag and listened to the old lady's thanks.

'You're off now?'

'Yes. I must take this young lady back to my aunt.'

'Come to dinner while you're there. We'd love to see

you again. How long are you here? Oslo, I suppose, and
Bergen and Tromsö?'

'Tromsö tomorrow,' said Mr Tait-Bouverie, 'and back
to England four days later.'

Kate had heard that, and was conscious of an unpleasant sensation under her ribs. Indigestion, she told herself,
and shook hands politely when Mr Tait-Bouverie intro-
duced her.

'This is not a social occasion, I am afraid, but I am
delighted to meet you—may I call you Kate? Perhaps next
time you come to Norway... Ah, here are the ambulance
men.' He smiled goodbye, and turned his attention to his
patient.

Mr Tait-Bouverie took Kate's hand. 'A hot bath and a
quiet evening,' he observed as they made their way
through the throng. Kate didn't reply. She would be lucky
if she had time for a quick shower; Lady Cowder wasn't
going to be pleased at having been kept waiting for more
than an hour...

It took some manoeuvring to get out of the tunnel; cars
were being backed, a way was being cleared by the police.
It was all very orderly, even if it took some time. The
road, when they at last reached it, had been closed to all
but traffic leaving the tunnel.

'It's all very efficiently organised,' said Kate.

Mr Tait-Bouverie glanced sideways at her. Her beautiful face was dirty and her hair, by now, a hopeless russet
tangle hanging down her back. He gave a sigh and kept
his eyes on the road.

He had been in love several times, just as any normal
man would be, but never once had he considered marriage. He had assumed that at sometime, somewhere, he
would meet the girl he wanted for his wife, and in the
meantime he immersed himself in his work, happy to

wait. Now he had found her and he didn't want to wait. He would have to, of course. He wasn't sure if she liked him—certainly she wasn't in love with him—and circumstances weren't going to make the prospect of that any easier. Circumstances, however, could be altered...

They talked about the accident presently. 'It is a miracle that it didn't turn into a major disaster...'

'You mean if fire had broken out or there had been panic? Everyone was calm. Well, nearly everyone.' Kate added honestly, 'I would have liked to have screamed, just once and very loudly, only I didn't dare.'

'Why not?'

She looked away from him out of the window. 'You wouldn't have liked that—I mean, you knew you would go and help. I dare say you would have left me in the car to scream all I wanted to, but you had enough on your plate.'

'I wouldn't have left you alone, Kate. To be truthful, I rather took it for granted that you would help, too, in your calm and sensible way.'

Kate fought a wish to tell him that she had felt neither of these things—that sheer fright had stricken her dumb. She had felt neither calm nor sensible, only terrified. Although she had to admit to herself that having him there, quiet and assured, knowing exactly what to do, had given her a feeling of safety. Strange to feel so safe and sure with him...

Soon they reached the hotel, and he got out and opened her door and walked with her into the foyer. There were a lot of people there, gathered to hear news of the accident, and they stared and then crowded round them, anxious for details.

'You were there?' someone asked. 'We felt sure that you were. The young lady...?'

'Is perfectly all right', said Mr Tait-Bouverie placidly. 'But she does need a bath and a rest.'

He took her to the desk and the three receptionists there hurried to him.

'Miss Crosby needs a bath, a change of clothing and a rest. I'm sure she'd like a tray of tea before anything else.' He looked at Kate. 'What is your room number? There is a bathroom?'

'Well, no,' she mumbled awkwardly. 'But the shower's fine. I'm perfectly all right.'

'Of course you are, but you will do what I say. Doctor's orders.'

He turned back to the desk. 'Will you send a chambermaid with Miss Crosby to fetch a change of clothes from her room, and then go with her to my room so that she may have a most essential warm bath? Perhaps she will let me know if Miss Crosby is bruised or scratched and I'll deal with that later. She is to stay with her, and I think that she might have dinner there. In the meantime let me have another room, will you?'

He said to Kate in what she could only call a doctor's voice, 'While you are finding something to wear I'll get what I need from my room. And here is the chambermaid. Go with her, and after your dinner go back to your room and go to bed.'

Kate found her voice. 'Lady Cowder…?'

'Leave her to me.' He smiled then, and she found herself smiling back and wanting to cry. 'Goodnight, Kate.'

She lay in the warm bath and snivelled. She didn't know why; she hadn't been hurt, only scratched and bruised, and was tired from the heaving and shoving and lifting she had done. But it was nice to have a good cry, and the chambermaid was a kindly soul who found plasters to put

on her small cuts and grazes and presently saw her onto
the bed and urged her to have a nice nap.

Which, surprisingly, she did, to wake feeling quite herself again and to eat with a splendid appetite the dinner
that the good soul brought to the room.

Kate had half expected to have a visit from Lady Cowder—or at least a message—but there was nothing. She
ate her dinner and, still accompanied by the chambermaid,
went back to her own room. In a little while she went to
bed. It was a pity that Mr Tait-Bouverie was going to
Tromsö tomorrow; she would have liked to thank him
properly for his kindness. She spared a sleepy moment to
wonder what he was doing...

He was walking briskly through the town, not going anywhere special, thinking about the afternoon and Kate. His
aunt had been vexed at the news that she would have to
manage without Kate that evening, declaring plaintively
that the news of the accident had been a great shock to
her, that she felt poorly and would probably have a mi-
graine.

To all of which Mr Tait-Bouverie had listened with his
usual courtesy, before suggesting that an early night might
be the answer.

'I'll say goodbye now, Aunt,' he had told her. 'For I'm
leaving early in the morning. I shall be back in England
shortly, and will come and see you as soon as you return.'

'I shall look forward to that, James. I believe that I shall
invite Claudia to stay for a while—she is such a splendid
companion, and so amusing.' When this had elicited no
response, she had added, 'How delightful it will be to see
your dear mother again. She wrote to say that she will be
returning soon. There is so much for us to talk about.'

Mr Tait-Bouverie considered his future with the same

thorough care with which he did his work. Complicated operations—the kind he excelled in—needed careful thought, and there would be plenty of complications before he could marry his Kate. At least, he reflected, he would know where she was...

Kate hadn't expected sympathy from Lady Cowder and she received none. 'So very inconvenient,' said that lady as Kate presented herself the following morning. 'You have no idea of the severity of my headache, and all the excitement about the accident... It was most generous of my nephew to give up his room for your use, though really quite unnecessary. However, he has always done as he wishes.'

Kate, perceiving that she was expected to answer this, said quietly, 'Mr Tait-Bouverie was very kind and considerate. I'm very grateful. I hope I shall have the opportunity of thanking him.'

'He wouldn't expect thanks from you,' said Lady Cowder rudely. 'Besides, he left early this morning for Tromsö. He will be back in England before us.'

Kate felt a pang of disappointment. Perhaps she would see him in England but on rather a different footing—the accident in the tunnel would have faded into the past, obliterated by a busy present. Thanking him would sound silly. She wondered if she should write him a polite note—but where would she send it? Lady Cowder could tell her, but she was the last person to ask. It was an unsatisfactory ending to what had been, for her, a very pleasant interlude, despite the fright and horror of the accident in the tunnel.

At least, Kate reflected, she had behaved sensibly even while her insides had heaved and she had been terrified that fire would break out or, worse, that the tunnel would fall apart above their heads and they would all be drowned. A flight of imagination, she knew. The tunnel was safe, and help had been prompt and more than efficient. It had been an experience—not a nice one, she had to admit—and despite her fright she had felt quite safe because Mr Tait-Bouverie had been there.

Waiting for Lady Cowder that afternoon, she wrote a long letter to her mother, making light of Lady Cowder's ill humour, describing the hotel and the town, the food and the people she had spoken to, enlarging on the beautiful scenery but saying little about Mr Tait-Bouverie's company. She wrote about the tunnel accident too, not dwelling on the horror of it, merely observing that it had been most fortunate that Mr Tait-Bouverie had been there to help.

She wrote nothing about her own part in the affair, hoping that her mother would picture her sitting safely in the car out of harm's way.

Her circumspection was wasted. Mrs Crosby, reading bits of the letter to Mr Tait-Bouverie, observed in a puzzled voice, 'But where was Kate? She doesn't say...'

They were sitting at the kitchen table, drinking coffee with Moggerty on Mr Tait-Bouverie's knee. He had arrived that afternoon, having driven down from London after a brief stop at his home. He'd been tired by the time his plane got in, and had hesitated as to whether it wouldn't be a better idea to go and see Kate's mother the following morning. But if Kate had written, the letter would have arrived by now and Mrs Crosby might be worried. He had eaten the meal Mudd had had ready for him and driven himself out of town, despite Mudd's disapproving look.

He was glad that he had come; Mrs Crosby had had

Play LUC

when you play
...then continu
with a sweethe

1. Play Lucky Hearts as instructed
2. Send back this card and you'll
   books have a cover price of $3.
   are yours to keep absolutely fre

3. There's no catch! You're under n
   ZERO—for your first shipment.
   of purchases—not even one!

4. The fact is thousands of readers
   Reader Service®. They enjoy the
   the best new novels at discount p
   love their *Heart to Heart* subscribe
   recipes, book reviews and much n

5. We hope that after receiving your f
   choice is yours—to continue or ca
   invitation, with no risk of any kind.

The Harlequin Reader Service®—Here's how it works:

Accepting your 2 free books and gift places you under no obligation to buy anything. You may keep the books and gift and return the shipping statement marked "cancel." If you do not cancel, about a month later we'll send you 6 additional novels and bill you just $2.90 each in the U.S., or $3.34 each in Canada, plus 25¢ shipping & handling per book and applicable taxes if any.* That's the complete price and — compared to cover prices of $3.50 each in the U.S. and $3.99 each in Canada — it's quite a bargain! You may cancel at any time, but if you choose to continue, every month we'll send you 6 more books, which you may either purchase at the discount price or return to us and cancel your subscription.

*Terms and prices subject to change without notice. Sales tax applicable in N.Y. Canadian residents will be charged applicable provincial taxes and GST.

the letter that morning and had been worrying about it ever since. He had been able to reassure her and tell her exactly what had happened. 'Kate behaved splendidly,' he told her. 'She's not easily rattled, is she?' He smiled a little. 'She didn't like the tunnel, though—too dark.'

Mrs Crosby offered Prince a biscuit. 'I'm glad she was able to help. Did Lady Cowder mind? I mean, Kate had to miss some of her duties, I expect.'

Mr Tait-Bouverie said soothingly, 'My aunt quite understood. Kate had her bath and her cuts and bruises were attended to, and she had an early night.'

'Oh, good. I shall be so glad to see her again, though it was most kind of Lady Cowder to take Kate with her. It's years since she had a holiday, and she does have to work hard.' She paused. 'I shouldn't have said that.'

Mr Tait-Bouverie offered Moggerty a finger to chew. 'Why not? Being a housekeeper to my aunt must be extremely hard work. You see, people who have never had to work themselves don't realise the amount of work other people do for them.'

'Well, yes, I dare say you're right. Are you not tired? It was very kind of you to come all this way... When do you start work again?'

'Tomorrow, and I knew that once I got started it would be some days before I could come and see you.'

'I'm very grateful. Kate's all right, isn't she? I mean, happy...?'

He said evenly, 'We had a very happy afternoon together. We went dancing one evening...she is a delightful dancer...'

'She was never without a partner at the parties she went to—that was before her father became ill. What was she wearing? She didn't take much with her—she didn't expect... Was it a brown dress?'

'I'm afraid so,' said Mr Tait-Bouverie gravely. 'She is far too beautiful to wear brown crêpe, Mrs Crosby.'

'She hadn't much choice,' said Mrs Crosby rather tartly.

'It made no difference,' he assured her. 'Kate would turn heads draped in a potato sack.'

Mrs Crosby met his unsmiling gaze and smiled. Not an idle remark calculated to please her, she decided. He really meant it.

He went away presently, with Prince at his heels eager to get into the car beside his master.

Mrs Crosby offered a hand. 'Don't work too hard,' she begged him. 'Though I suppose that in a job like yours you can't very well say no...'

He laughed then. 'That's true, but I do get the odd free day or weekend. I hope I may be allowed to come and see you from time to time?'

'That would be delightful.'

She watched him drive away, wondering if his visit had been made out of concern for her worry about Kate or because he really wanted to see her—and Kate—in the future. 'We shall have to wait and see,' she told Moggerty.

Kate quickly discovered that she was to pay for the few hours of pleasure she had had with Mr Tait-Bouverie. Lady Cowder declared that she was tired of bridge, and on fine afternoons a car was hired and she and Kate were driven around the countryside—Kate sitting with the driver since Lady Cowder declared that Kate's chatter gave her a headache.

Kate ignored this silly remark, and was thankful to sit beside the driver, who pointed out anything interesting and, before long, told her about his wife and children.

After several days of this the weather changed and, instead of going out in the afternoons, Lady Cowder stayed in one of the hotel lounges, playing patience or working away at a jigsaw puzzle while Kate sat quietly by, ready to help with the patience when it wouldn't come out, or grovel around the floor looking for lost bits of the puzzle.

Now she had only a brief hour each morning to herself, so the days stretched endlessly in long, wasted hours.

It was only during the last few days of their stay that this dull routine was altered, when Lady Cowder decided to shop for presents. She hadn't many friends—bridge-playing acquaintances for the most part—and for those she bought carved woodwork. But Claudia was a different matter.

'Something special for the dear girl,' she told Kate. 'She is so pretty; one must choose something to enhance that. Earrings, I think—those rather charming gold and silver filigree drops I saw yesterday. Of course, they are of no value; James will see that she has some good jewellery when they marry...'

She shot a look at Kate as she spoke, but was answered with a noncommittal, 'They would be charming. I'm sure Claudia will be delighted to have them.'

'Such a grateful girl. You might do better to copy her gratitude, Kate.'

Kate, with a tremendous effort, held her tongue!

The journey back to England went smoothly—largely because Kate had planned it to be so. All the same, it was tiring work getting Lady Cowder out of cars, into the plane and out of it again and then into her own car. She had complained gently the whole way home so that Kate had a headache by the time they stopped in front of Lady Cowder's house.

That was when her long day's work really started.

Safely home again, Lady Cowder declared that she was exhausted and must go to bed at once.

'You may bring in the luggage and unpack, Kate, but before you do that bring a tray of tea up to my room. I'll take a warm bath and go to bed, I think, and later you may bring me up a light supper.' She sighed. 'How I envy you your youth and strength—when one is old...'

Seventy wasn't all that old, reflected Kate, receiving an armful of handbags, scarves and rugs. And Lady Cowder lived the kind of life which was conducive to looking and feeling a lot younger than one's years. She saw Lady Cowder to her room, got her bath ready and went downstairs to unload the boot.

Lady Cowder was in bed by the time Kate had put the car away and brought the luggage indoors.

'You might as well unpack my things now,' said Lady Cowder, sitting up against her pillows as fresh as a daisy.

'If I do,' said Kate in her quiet voice, 'I won't have time to get your supper.' She added woodenly, 'I could cut you a few sandwiches...'

Lady Cowder closed her eyes. 'After my very tiring day I need a nourishing meal. Leave the unpacking, since you don't seem capable of doing it this evening. A little soup, I think, and a lamb chop with a few peas—if there are none in the freezer, I dare say you can get them from the garden. Just one or two potatoes, plainly boiled. I don't suppose you will have time to make a compote of fruit; I had better make do with an egg custard.' She opened her eyes. 'In about an hour, Kate.'

Only the thought of the extra wages she had earned, enough—just—to make up the hundred pounds to show the bank manager, kept Kate from picking up her unopened bags and going home.

She went to the kitchen, put on the kettle and made tea,

then a little refreshed but still angry, she phoned her mother.

'I can't stop,' she told her. 'There's rather a lot to do, but I'll see you on Wednesday. I'm to go to Thame for some groceries on Thursday; I'll go to the bank then.'

Her mother's happy voice did much to cheer her up— after all, it had been worth it; the rather grey future held a tinge of pink. In a few months she would be embarking on a venture which she felt sure would be successful.

Later she carried a beautifully cooked meal up to Lady Cowder's room.

'You may fetch the tray when I ring,' said that lady. 'Then I shan't need anything more. I'll have breakfast as usual up here. Poached eggs on toast, and some of that marmalade from the Women's Institute. In the New Year you can make sufficient for the whole year; I cannot enjoy any of these marmalades from the shops.'

Kate said, 'Goodnight, Lady Cowder,' and received no answer. She hadn't expected one. She hadn't expected to be asked if she were at all tired or hungry, nor had she expected to be thanked for her services during their stay in Norway. But it would have been nice to have been treated like a person and not like a robot.

She ate her supper, unpacked her things, had a very long, too hot bath and then went to bed. She was tired, but not too tired to wonder what Mr Tait-Bouverie was doing. She told herself sleepily not to waste time thinking about him and went to sleep.

She was kept busy the next day; after a month's emptiness the house was clean, but it needed dusting and airing. Stores had to be checked, tradesmen phoned, the gardener had to be seen about vegetables, and Horace to be made much of. He had been well looked after but he was glad of her company again, and followed her round the house, anxious to please.

Lady Cowder, catching sight of him following Kate up the stairs, said irritably, 'What is that cat doing here? I thought he had been got rid of. I'm sure I told Mrs Beckett to have him put down before she left...'

'It's most fortunate that she didn't, Lady Cowder,' said Kate in the polite voice which so annoyed her employer. 'For he is splendid at catching mice. All those small rooms behind the kitchen which are never used...he never allows one to get away.'

She uttered the fib with her fingers crossed behind her back. It was a fib in a good cause—Horace was a sympathetic companion and someone to talk to. That he had never caught a mouse in his life had nothing to do with it...

'Mice?' said Lady Cowder in horror. 'You mean to tell me...?'

'No, no. There are no mice, but there might be without Horace. A cat,' she went on in her sensible way, 'is of much more use than a mousetrap.'

Lady Cowder agreed grudgingly, annoyed to feel that Kate had got the better of her without uttering a single word which could be described as impertinent or rude.

Kate went home on her half-day, taking her extra wages with her, and she and her mother spent a blissful afternoon making plans for the future.

'I'll need a thousand pounds to start,' said Kate. 'I'll start in a small way, and then get the money paid off to the bank and get better equipment as we expand. I'll stay with Lady Cowder until I've drummed up one or two customers—the pub, perhaps, and that bed and breakfast place at the other end of the village. Once I can get regular customers I can branch out—birthday parties and even weddings...'

'It's something you can go on doing if you marry,' observed her mother.

'Yes, but I don't know anyone who wants to marry me, do I?' For some reason Mr Tait-Bouverie's face rose, unbidden, beneath her eyelids and she added, 'And I'm not likely to.'

She took care to laugh as she said it and her mother smiled in return—but her eyes were thoughtful. Mr Tait-Bouverie would make a delightful son-in-law, and he might fall in love with Kate. It didn't seem likely, but Mrs Crosby was an optimist by nature.

Before Kate went back that evening she arranged to call in the next day on her way to Thame. She wasn't to use the car—Lady Cowder considered that Kate could cycle there and back quite easily with the few dainties which she had set her heart on.

'I quite envy you,' she'd told Kate in the wistful voice which made Kate clench her teeth. 'Young and strong with the whole morning for a pleasant little outing.'

Kate said nothing. The bike ride was one thing, but shopping around for the special mushrooms, the oysters, the lamb's sweetbreads, the special sauce which could only be found at a delicatessen some distance from the shopping centre was quite another. But she didn't mind; she was going to find time to go to the bank...

Kate got up earlier than usual, for Lady Cowder expected the morning's chores to be done before she left, but still Kate left the house later than she had hoped for. It would be a bit of a rush to get back in time to get Lady Cowder's lunch. She stayed at her home only long enough to collect the hundred pounds, which she stowed in her shoulderbag and slung over her shoulder. It would never do to get it mixed up with the housekeeping money in the bike's basket, every penny of which she would have to account for.

It was a dull day, but she didn't mind that—this was the day she had been working and waiting for. Now she could plan her future, a successful career... It was a pity that Mr Tait-Bouverie's handsome features kept getting in the way.

'Forget him,' said Kate loudly. 'Just because he was kind and nice to be with. Remember, you're a housekeeper!'

She bowled along, deciding what to do first—the bank or the shopping. Would she be a long time at the bank? Would she be able to see the manager at once? Perhaps she should have made an appointment. Another mile or so and she would be on the outskirts of Thame. She would go to the bank first...

She parked her bike and had turned round to take her shopping bag and the housekeeping money from the basket when she was jostled by several youths. They did it quite roughly, treading on her feet, pushing her against the wall, but before she could do anything they chorused loud apologies—presumably for the benefit of the few pedestrians in the street—and ran away.

They took her shoulderbag with them, neatly sliced from its straps.

It had all happened so quickly that she had no chance to look at them properly. There had been four or five of them, she thought, and she ran across the street to ask if anyone passing had seen what had happened. No one had, although they admitted that they had thought the boys had bumped into her accidentally.

So she went into the bank, calm with despair, and explained that her money had been stolen. Here she was listened to with sympathy, given an offer to phone the police, and told with polite regret that an interview with the manager would be pointless until the money was recovered. When a police officer arrived there was little he could do, although he assured her that they would certainly be on the look-out for the youths.

'Although I doubt if you'll see your money back, miss,' she was told.

She gave her name and address, assured him that she was unharmed and, since there was nothing else to be done about it, got on her bike and did her shopping. A pity that they hadn't taken the housekeeping money instead of her precious savings.

She didn't allow herself to think about it while she shopped. Her world had fallen around her in ruins, and she would have to start to rebuild it all over again. Disappointment tasted bitter in her mouth, but for the moment there were more important things to think of. Lady Cowder's lunch, for instance...

She cycled back presently, her purchases made, wondering how she was going to break the news to her mother. She would have to wait until Sunday. She rarely got the chance to use the phone unless it was on Lady Cowder's behalf, and she saw no hope of getting enough free time to go home until then. And she had no intention of telling Lady Cowder.

Back at the house, she was reprimanded in Lady Cowder's deceptively gentle voice for being late. 'It is so essential that I should have my meals served punctually,' she pointed out. 'I feel quite low, and now I must wait for lunch to be served. You may pour me a glass of sherry, Kate.'

Which Kate did in calm silence before going down to

the kitchen to deal with the mushrooms and oysters. But before she did that she poured herself a glass of the cooking sherry—an inferior brand, of course, but still sherry.

She tossed it off recklessly and started on her preparations for lunch, not caring if she burnt everything to cinders or curdled the sauce. Of course, she didn't; she served a beautifully cooked meal to an impatient Lady Cowder and went back to the kitchen where she sat down and had a good cry.

CHAPTER SIX

KATE felt better in the morning. The loss was a set-back, but with the optimism born of a new day she told herself that a hundred pounds wasn't such a vast sum and if she could save it once, she could save it a second time.

Her optimism faded as the day wore on; Lady Cowder was demanding, and for some reason sorry for herself. She declared that the journey home had upset her and went round the house finding fault with everything.

It was a blessing when the vicar's wife called after lunch to confer with her about the Autumn Fair. Lady Cowder prided herself on patronising local charity, and made no bones about telling everyone how generous she was in their cause.

She spent a pleasant afternoon telling the vicar's wife just how things should be done. Kate, bringing in the tea tray, heard her telling that lady that she would be delighted to supply as many cakes and biscuits as were needed for the cake stall and the refreshment tent.

'As you know,' said Lady Cowder in her wispy voice, 'I will go to any amount of trouble to help a worthy cause.'

Kate, with the prospect of hours of cake baking ahead of her, sighed.

The vicar's wife was only a passing respite, though; by the following morning Lady Cowder was as gloomy as

ever. Thank heavens, thought Kate, that I can go home
tomorrow.

Lady Cowder fancied a sponge cake for her tea. 'Although I dare say I shall eat only a morsel of it.' She
added sharply, 'Any of the cake which is left over you
may use for a trifle, Kate.'

Kate stood there, not saying a word, her face calm, and
wearing the air of reserve which annoyed her employer.
'I'll have the turbot with wild mushrooms for dinner. Oh,
and a spinach salad, I think, and a raspberry tart with
orange sauce.' She glanced at Kate. 'You're rather pale.
I hope you aren't going to be ill, Kate.'

'I'm very well, thank you,' said Kate, and went away
to make the sponge cake. She hoped it would turn out like
lead, but as usual it was as light as a feather.

She thought of Mr Tait-Bouverie as she worked. It was
silly of her to waste time over him, but at least it stopped
her thinking about her lost money.

Mr Tait-Bouverie stood at the window, looking at his
aunt's garden. He wasn't sure why he had felt the urge to
pay her a visit and had no intention of pursuing the matter
too deeply. He had almost convinced himself that the feelings he had for Kate were nothing more than a passing
infatuation, but when the door opened and she came in
with the tea tray he had to admit that that was nonsense.
Nothing less than marrying her would do, and that as soon
as possible.

However, he let none of these feelings show but bade
her a quiet good afternoon and watched her arrange the
tray to please his aunt. She had gone delightfully pink
when she'd seen him, but now he saw that she looked
pale and tired. More than that—unhappy.

She left the room as quietly as she had entered, not

looking at him again, aware of Lady Cowder's sharp eyes, and he went to take his tea cup from his aunt and sit down opposite her.

'I'm sorry to hear that you found the journey home tiring. Kate looks tired, too. Perhaps you should have broken your trip and stayed in town for a night.'

'My dear boy, all I longed to do was get here—and indeed the journey was so fatiguing, getting to the airport and then the flight. You know how nervous I am. And then standing about while the luggage is seen to and the car fetched—and then the long drive here.' She added sharply, 'Kate isn't in the least tired. She's a great strapping girl, perfectly able to cope—and after a month's idleness, too. I'm glad to see that she hasn't taken advantage of your kindness to her at Alesund.'

Mr Tait-Bouverie gave her a look of such coldness that she shivered.

'Of course, I'm sure she would do no such thing,' she said hastily. 'Such a reserved young woman.' Anxious to take the look of ferocity from her nephew's face, she added, 'You will stay to dinner, won't you, James?'

Mr Tait-Bouverie, making plans, declined. After his absence from London, he pointed out, he had a backlog of work. He urged his aunt to take more exercise, volunteered to let himself out of the house and went round to the kitchen door.

Kate was sitting at the table. The ingredients for the raspberry tart Lady Cowder fancied for dinner were before her, although she was making no attempt to do anything about it.

Seeing Mr Tait-Bouverie had been a bit of a shock—a surprisingly pleasant one, she discovered. She had put down the tea tray and taken care to reply to his pleasant greeting with suitable reserve, but the urge to fall on his neck and pour out her troubles had been very strong. She reflected that she must like him more than she thought she did, not that her feelings came into it.

'But it would be nice to have a shoulder to moan on,' she observed to Horace, who was sitting cosily by the Aga.

'I don't know if you have a shoulder in mind,' said Mr Tait-Bouverie from the door. 'But would mine do?'

She turned her head to look at him. 'You shouldn't creep up on people like that; it's bad for the nerves.'

Indeed, she had gone very pale at the sight of him.

He came right into the room and sat down at the table opposite her.

'Did I shock you? I'm sorry. Now tell me, Kate, what is the matter? And don't waste time saying nothing, because neither you nor I have time to waste.'

'I have no intention...' began Kate, and stopped when she caught his eye. She said baldly, 'I went to Thame on Thursday to shop, you know, and I had the money—the hundred pounds—with me to take to the bank. I was going to see the manager. I was mugged by some boys. They took my bag with the money inside.' She paused to look at him. 'Fortunately the housekeeping money was in the basket on my bike, so I was able to do the shopping.'

She managed a small smile. 'I'm a bit disappointed.'

He put out a hand and took hers, which was lying on the table, in his. 'My poor Kate. What a wretched thing to happen. Of course, you told the police...?'

'Yes. They said they'd do their best—but, you see, no one really saw it happen. People were passing on the other side of the street but not looking, if you see what I mean.'

'You told my aunt?'

She gave her hand a tug but he held it fast. 'Well, no; there's no point in doing that, is there?'

'Your mother?'

'It's my free day tomorrow. I shall tell her then.'

'What do you intend to do?'

'Why, start again, of course. I'd hoped that I would be able to leave here quite soon, but now I'll stay for at least a year—if Lady Cowder wants me to.' Her voice wobbled a bit at the thought of that, but she added, 'A year isn't long.'

Mr Tait-Bouverie got up, came round the table, heaved her gently out of her chair and took her in his arms. He did it in the manner in which she might have expected a brother or a favourite uncle would do. Kind and impersonal, and bracingly sympathetic. It cost him an effort, but he loved her.

It was exactly what Kate needed—a shoulder to cry on—and she did just that, comforted by his arms, soothed by his silence. She cried for quite some time, but presently gave a great sniff and mumbled, 'Sorry about that. I feel much better now. I've soaked your jacket.'

He handed her a beautifully laundered handkerchief. 'Have a good blow,' he advised. 'There's nothing like a good weep to clear the air. What time are you free tomorrow?'

'I usually get away just after nine o'clock, unless Lady Cowder needs something at the last minute.'

'I'll be outside at half past nine to take you home. It might help your mother if I'm there, and it might be easier for you to explain. She's bound to be upset.'

'Yes.' Kate mopped her face and blew her pink nose again. 'That would be very kind of you, but are you staying here for the night? I didn't know——I must make up a bed...'

'I'm going back home now.' He gave her a kind and what he hoped was an avuncular smile. 'I'll be here in the morning. Perhaps we can think of something to help your mother over her disappointment. Now cheer up, Kate; something will turn up...'

'What?' asked Kate.

'Well, that's the nice part about it, because you don't know, do you? And a surprise is always exciting.' He bent and kissed her cheek. 'I must go. See you in the morning. And, Kate—sleep well tonight.'

She nodded. 'I think I shall. And thank you, Mr Tait-Bouverie, you have been so kind.' She smiled. 'You're quite right; there's nothing like a good weep on some-one's shoulder. I'm grateful for yours.'

She sat at the table for several minutes after he had gone. He had offered no solution, made no hopeful sug-gestions, and yet she felt cheerful about the future. Per-haps it was because he had been so matter-of-fact about it, while at the same time accepting her bout of weeping with just the right amount of calm sympathy. Breaking the news to her mother would be a great deal easier with him there.

He had kissed her, too. A light, brotherly kiss which had made her feel...she sought for the right word. Cher-ished. Absurd, of course.

She got up and began to prepare Lady Cowder's dinner, then made herself a pot of tea, gave Horace his evening snack and sat down again to wait for Lady Cowder's ring signalling her wish for her dinner to be served.

It was a fine morning when Kate woke from a good night's sleep. A pity her nicest dress had been ruined in the tunnel she thought as she got into a cotton jersey dress. It had been a pretty blue once upon a time, but constant washing had faded it. As she fastened its belt she wished that she had something pretty and fashionable to wear, and then told herself not to be silly; Mr Tait-Bouverie wouldn't notice what she was wearing.

He did, however, down to the last button, while watching her coming round the side of the house from the kitchen door, the sun shining on her glorious hair, smiling at him shyly because she felt awkward at the remembrance of her tears yesterday.

He wished her good morning, popped her into the car and drove off without waste of time. 'Your mother won't mind Prince again?' he wanted to know.

'No, of course not; he's such a dear.' She turned round to look at him sitting at the back, grinning at her with his tongue hanging out.

'You have slept,' observed Mr Tait-Bouverie.

'Yes, yes, I did. I'm sorry I was so silly yesterday—I was tired...' She glanced at his rather stern profile. 'Please forget it.'

He didn't answer as he stopped before her home, but got out and opened her door and let Prince out to join them. By the time he had done that Mrs Crosby was at the open door.

'What a lovely surprise. Hello, darling, and how delightful to see you again, Mr Tait-Bouverie. I hope you've come to stay? There's coffee all ready—we can have it in the garden.'

She beamed at them both and stooped to pat Prince. 'You'll stay?' she asked again.

'With pleasure, Mrs Crosby. You don't mind Prince?'

'Of course not. He shall have some water and a biscuit.' She turned to Kate. 'Go into the garden, dear, I'll bring the tray...'

Mr Tait-Bouverie carried the tray out while Kate

fetched the little queen cakes her mother had made, all the while talking over-brightly about Norway—indeed, hardly pausing for breath, so anxious was she not to have a long silence which might encourage her mother to ask about her trip to Thame.

In the end, Mrs Crosby managed to get a word in. She couldn't ask outright about the bank manager, not in front of their guest, but she asked eagerly, 'Did you have a successful trip to Thame, dear?'

'I've some disappointing news, mother,' began Kate.

'Won't they lend you the money? Wasn't it enough, the hundred pounds?'

'Well, mother, I didn't get the chance to find out. I was mugged just outside the bank. The police don't think that there is much chance of getting the money back—it was in my bag.'

Mrs Crosby put her cup carefully back into the saucer. She had gone rather pale. 'You mean, there is no money…?'

'I'm afraid not, Mother, dear. It's a bit of a blow, isn't it? But we'll just have to start again.'

'You mean,' said Mrs Crosby unhappily, 'that you must go on working like a slave for too little money for another year? More, perhaps.'

She picked up her cup and put it down again because her hand was shaking. 'Did you know about this?' she asked Mr Tait-Bouverie.

'Yes, Mrs Crosby. I saw Kate yesterday evening and she told me.'

Mrs Crosby said, 'I can quite understand what a relief it must be to have hysterics. Kate, dear, I am so very sorry. After all these months of work—and you've never once complained.' She looked at Mr Tait-Bouverie. 'This is rather dull for you. Let's talk about something else.'

He said in his calm way, 'If I might make a suggestion, there is perhaps something to be done...'

He had spent a large amount of the previous evening on the telephone after he'd returned home, but first of all he had gone in search of Mudd, who had been sitting in the comfortable kitchen doing the crossword.

'Mudd, do I pay you an adequate wage?'

Mudd had got to his feet and been told to sit down again. 'Indeed, you do, sir; slightly more than is the going rate.'

'Oh, good. Tell me, would you know the—er—going rate for a housekeeper? One who runs the house more or less single-handed and does all the cooking.'

'A good plain cook or cordon bleu?' asked Mudd.

'Oh, cordon bleu.'

Mudd thought, named a sum and added, 'Such a person would expect her own quarters too, the use of the car, two days off a week and annual holiday.'

Mudd looked enquiringly at Mr Tait-Bouverie, but if he hoped to hear more he was to be disappointed. He was thanked and left to his puzzle while Mr Tait-Bouverie went to his study and sat down at his desk to think. The half-formed plan he had allowed to simmer as he drove himself home began to take shape. Presently, when it came to the boil, he had picked up the phone and dialled a number.

Now he returned Kate's look of suspicion with a bland stare. 'No, Kate, it isn't something I've thought up during the last few minutes. It is something I remembered on my way home last night. An old lady—an extremely active eighty-something—told me some time ago that her cook would have to go into hospital for some time and would probably be away for several months. It seems the poor woman should have been there much earlier, but her employer was unable to find someone to replace her. She lives in a village south of Bath—a large house, well staffed... Kate, will you tell me what wages you receive?'

She told him, for she saw no reason not to.

'I believe that you are underpaid by my aunt. Did you know that?'

'Oh, yes. But I needed a job badly, and someone we knew offered us this cottage at a cheap rent. I know I'm not paid enough, but where would I find another job where we could live as cheaply as we do here?'

'Exactly. But if you could get work where you lived rent-free and were better paid, it might be a good idea to take a calculated risk. You would be able to save more money—no rent, nor gas or electricity. I'm a bit vague about such things, but surely there would be more scope for saving?'

'But it would be temporary. I might be out of work again...'

He raised his eyebrows. 'With Bath only four miles away?' He smiled. 'Faint-hearted, Kate?'

She flared up. 'Certainly not; what a horrid thing to say.' She added quickly, 'I'm sorry. That was ungrateful and horrid of me.'

She looked at her mother. Mrs Crosby said quietly, 'We have nothing to lose, have we? I think it's a marvellous idea, and I'm grateful to James...' She smiled across at him. 'You don't mind? You see, I feel that you are our friend...for thinking of it and offering us help.'

Kate got up and went to stand by his chair, and when he got up, too, held out her hand. 'Mother's right; you're being kind and helping us, and I don't deserve it. I feel awful about it.'

He took her hand in his and smiled down at her. 'I hope that I may always be your friend, Kate—you and your mother. And as for being kind, I don't need to trouble myself further than to write to this old lady and let you know what she says. She may, of course, have already found someone to her taste.'

All of which sounded very convincing in Kate's ear. As he had meant it to.

Kate took her hand away reluctantly. 'What do you want us to do? Write to this lady asking her if she will employ me?'

'No, no. I think it best if I write to her and discover if she has found someone already. If she has, there is no more to be said—but if she is still seeking someone, I could suggest that I know of a good cook who would be willing to take over for as long as is needed.' He looked at Mrs Crosby. 'Would that do, do you suppose?'

'Very well, I should think. We'll try and forget about it until we hear from you, then we shan't be disappointed.' She smiled at him. 'We can never thank you enough, James. I've said that already, but I must say it again.'

He went away soon after that, leaving them to speculate about a possible future. 'James is quite right,' said Mrs Crosby. 'If we can live rent-free think of the money we'll save. Even if the job lasts for only a few months we might have enough to get started, with help from the bank.'

'It's a risk.'

'Worth taking,' said Mrs Crosby cheerfully, and clinched the matter.

Kate heard nothing from Mr Tait-Bouverie for the best part of a week and then suddenly there he was, standing in the kitchen doorway, wishing her good afternoon in a cool voice.

Kate paused in her pastry making, aware of pleasure at seeing him.

'Are you staying for dinner?' she wanted to know. 'Because if you are I'll have to grill some more lamb chops.'

'No. No. I merely called in on my way back from Bristol. I have been sent by my aunt to tell you that I am here for tea.'

'I have just taken an apple cake out of the oven. Does Lady Cowder want tea at once?'

'I do have to leave in half an hour or so, if that is not too much trouble?'

He came further into the kitchen. 'I heard from the old lady I told you about. She will be writing to you. It will be for you to decide what you want to do, Kate.'

She smiled widely at him. 'You have? She will write? That's marvellous news. Thank you, Mr Tait-Bouverie. If this lady wants me to work for her I'll go there as soon as I've given notice here.' She added uncertainly, 'If she would wait?'

'Oh, I imagine so,' said Mr Tait-Bouverie easily. 'I don't suppose another week or so will make any difference.'

He strolled to the door. 'I'm sure everything will get nicely settled without any difficulties.'

He had gone before she could thank him.

The letter came the next day. Kate was asked to present herself for an interview on a day suitable to herself during the next week, and she wrote back at once, suggesting the following Wednesday afternoon.

Getting there might be a problem—one solved by asking the son of the owner of the village shop to give her a lift into Oxford, where she could catch a train. It would be a tiresome journey, and to be on the safe side she told Lady Cowder that she might be back late in the evening.

Kate, hurrying down to the village to start her journey

on Wednesday afternoon, felt mean about leaving Lady Cowder in the dark—then she remembered how that lady hadn't scrupled to underpay her...

Rather to her surprise, she was to be met at Bath and driven to her prospective employer's house, which was at a small village some four miles or so away. The man who met her was elderly and very polite, although he offered no information about himself.

'Mrs Braithewaite is elderly, miss, as you perhaps know. You are to see her first for a short interview and then have a talk with Cook. You are to return to Thame this evening?'

'Yes. I hope to catch the half-past-six train to Oxford if possible.'

'I shall be taking you back to Bath. You should be finished by then.'

He had no more to say, and sat silently until he turned in at an open gate and drew up before an imposing Queen Anne house set in a large garden. Its massive front door was flanked by rows of large windows, but Kate followed her companion round the side of the house and went in through a side door.

The kitchen at the end of the stone passage was large and airy and, she noted, well equipped with a vast Aga and a huge dresser, rows of saucepans on its walls and a solid table. There were chairs each side of the Aga and a tabby cat curled up in one of them. There were three people there—an elderly woman, sitting on one of the chairs, and two younger women at the table, drinking tea.

They looked up as Kate was ushered in, and the elder woman said, 'You're young, but from all accounts you're a good cook. Sit down and have a cup of tea. Mrs Braithewaite will see you in ten minutes. I'm Mrs Willett. This is Daisy, the housemaid, and Meg, the kitchenmaid. Mr Tombs, the butler, will see you before you go.'

Kate accepted a cup of tea, thanked the man who had driven her from the station and got a quick nod from him. 'I'm the chauffeur and gardener; Briggs is the name.'

'I'm very grateful for the lift.'

He shrugged. 'It's my job. You don't look much like a cook, miss.'

She was saved from answering this by Mrs Willett, who got to her feet with some difficulty, saying, 'Time we went.'

They went along a lengthy passage and through a door opening into the entrance hall. They crossed this and Mrs Willett knocked on one of the several doors opening from it. Bidden to come in, she stood aside for Kate to go in and then followed her to stand by the door.

'Come here.' The old lady sitting in a high-backed chair by the window had a loud, commanding voice. 'Where I can see you. What's your name again?'

'Kate Crosby, Mrs Braithewaite.'

'Hmm. I'm told you can cook. Is that true?'

'Yes. I can cook.'

'It's a temporary job, you understand that? While Mrs Willett has time off to go to hospital and convalesce. I have no idea how long that will be, but you'll be given reasonable notice. Dependants?'

'My mother.'

'There's Mrs Willett's cottage at the back of the house. She's willing for you to live there while she's away. Bring your mother if you wish. I take it you have references? I know Mr Tait-Bouverie recommended you, but I want references as well.'

Kate had a chance to study the old lady as she spoke. Stout, and once upon a time a handsome woman, even now she was striking, with white hair beautifully dressed. She wore a great many chains and rings and there was a stick by her chair.

'I'm a difficult person to please,' went on Mrs Braithewaite. 'I'll stand no nonsense. Do your work well and you will be well treated and paid. You can start as soon as possible. Arrange that with Mrs Willett.'

Mrs Willett gave a little cough which Kate rightly took to be a signal to take her leave.

She thanked Mrs Braithewaite politely, bade her good day and followed Mrs Willett out of the room.

'There, that's settled, then,' said the cook in a relieved voice. 'You've no idea how many she's interviewed, and me just dying to get to hospital and be seen to.'

'I'll come as soon as I can. I have to give notice where I'm working at present. I'll write to you as soon as I've got a date to leave, shall I?'

'You do that, miss. What's your name again? Not married, are you?'

'No. Would you call me Kate?'

'Suits me. I'll tell the others. Come and see the cottage, and there's time for another cup of tea before Briggs takes you back. And you've still got to see Mr Tombs.'

The cottage was close to the house—a small, rather sparsely furnished living room opened into a minuscule kitchen and a further door led to a bathroom. The stairs, behind a door in the sitting room wall, led to two bedrooms, each with a single bed, dressing table and clothes cupboard.

Kate said, 'We have our own furniture where we are at present. We'll store it, of course, but would you like us to bring our own bed linen—and anything else to replace whatever you would like to pack away? We're careful tenants…'

Mrs Willett looked pleased. 'Now that's a nice idea, Kate. Bring your own sheets and table linen. I'll put anything I want to store away in the cupboard in the living room.'

'There's just one other thing—we have a cat. He's elderly and well-behaved.'

'Suits me, so long as he doesn't mess up my things.' Mrs Willett led the way back to the house. 'Mr Tombs will be waiting to see you...'

Mr Tombs was an imposing figure of a man. Middle-aged, with strands of hair carefully combed over his balding pate, he wore a severe expression and an air of self-importance. He fixed her with a cold eye and expressed the wish that they would suit each other. 'The kitchen is, of course, your domain, but all household matters must be referred to me,' he told her pompously.

Later, in the car being driven back to her train, Briggs said, 'You don't have to worry about Mr Tombs; his bark's worse than his bite.'

'Thank you for telling me,' said Kate. 'But I shan't have much to do with the house, shall I? And the kitchen, as he said, is to be my domain.' She added, 'I think I'm quite easy to get on with.'

That sounded a bit cocksure. 'I mean, I'll try to fit in as quickly as possible, and I hope that someone will tell me if I don't. I shall do my best to do as Mrs Willett has done.'

'No doubt. We're all that glad that Mrs Willett can get seen to. She's waited long enough.'

Presently he left her at the station and she got into the train and spent the journey back making plans. They would have to start packing up, and the furniture would have to be stored, but they would be able to take some of their small possessions, she supposed. There was the question of telling Lady Cowder, too.

Kate spent a long time rehearsing what she would say. By the time she reached Oxford she was word-perfect.

Jimmy from the village had promised to meet her, and he was waiting.

'Any luck?' he wanted to know.

'Yes, I've got the job—but don't tell a soul until I've given in my notice, will you?'

'Course not. Coming back here when the job's finished?'

'Well, I don't know. Perhaps, if we can have the cottage back again.'

He left her at her home with a cheerful goodnight and she quickly went indoors to tell her mother. 'I can't stop,' she told her. 'I'll tell you all about it on Sunday. I've got the job. I'll have to give in my notice tomorrow.'

She kissed her mother, got on her bike and pedalled back to Lady Cowder's house. It was late now, and she would be hauled over the coals in the morning in Lady Cowder's gentle, complaining voice. She let herself in, crept up to her room and, once in bed, lay worrying about the morning. She expected an unpleasant interview and the prospect allowed her only brief snatches of sleep.

Her forebodings looked as if they were going to come true, for when she took in Lady Cowder's tea that lady said, 'I wish to speak to you after breakfast, Kate. Come to my sitting room at ten o'clock.'

Kate, outwardly her usual quiet, composed self was very surprised to find Lady Cowder looking uneasy when she presented herself. She didn't look at Kate, but kept her eyes on the book on her lap.

'Yesterday I had a long talk with my god-daughter,

Claudia—Miss Travers. As you know, I am devoted to her. She told me that her mother is going to live in the south of France and is dismissing her staff at her home here in England. Claudia is upset, since their housekeeper has been with them for some years and is, in her opinion, too elderly to find another post. Claudia asked me— begged me—to employ this woman.

'Claudia is a sensible girl as well as a strikingly pretty one—she pointed out that it will be easier for you to obtain a new post than their own housekeeper, and suggested that you might consider leaving. She is quite right, of course.' Lady Cowder looked up briefly. 'So be good enough to take a week's notice as from today, Kate. I will, of course, give you an excellent reference.'

Kate restrained herself from dancing a jig; indeed, she didn't allow her surprised delight to show. Lady Cowder's discomfiture was very evident, and Kate added to it with her calm, 'Very well, Lady Cowder. Have you decided what you would like for lunch today? And will there be your usual bridge tea this afternoon?'

'Yes, yes, of course. I have no appetite—an omelette with a salad will do.'

Kate shut the door quietly as she went, and then danced all the way down to the kitchen, where she gave Horace the contents of a tin of sardines and made herself coffee. She couldn't quite believe this sudden quirk of fate, but she was thankful for it. It was a good sign, she told herself; the future was going to be rosy. Well, perhaps not quite that, but certainly pink-tinged.

She would have to write to Mr Tait-Bouverie and tell him that his help had borne fruit. She knew where he worked as a consultant, for her mother had asked him, and she would send a letter there.

She composed it while she assembled Lady Cowder's

coffee tray. She wasn't likely to see him again, she reflected, and felt decidedly sad at the thought. 'Which is silly,' she told Horace, 'for we quite often disagree, although he can be very kind and—and safe, if you know what I mean. Only I wish he wasn't going to marry Claudia…'

She wrote the letter that evening and gave it to Mrs Pickett to post when she went home. It had been surprisingly difficult to write; things she wanted to tell him and which would have sounded all right if she had uttered them looked silly on paper. She considered the final effort very satisfactory, and had stamped it with the feeling that she had sealed away part of her life instead of just the envelope. She had no reason to feel sad, she reminded herself, and the concern she felt for his forthcoming marriage to Claudia was quite unnecessary—in fact, rather silly.

Mr Tait-Bouverie read the letter as he ate his breakfast the following morning. Reading its stiff contents, he reflected that Kate must have had a bad time composing it. It held no warmth but expressed very correctly her gratitude, her wish for his pleasant future and an assurance that she would endeavour to please her new employer. No one reading the letter would have recognised the Kate who wrote it—but, of course, Mr Tait-Bouverie, with a wealth of memories, even the most trivial ones, tucked away in his clever head, knew better. He read it again and then folded it carefully and put it into his pocket. Kate might think that they would never meet again but he knew better than that.

CHAPTER SEVEN

THERE was a great deal to do during the next few days, but Lady Cowder rather surprisingly told Kate that she might go home each evening after she had served dinner and cleared away the dishes. Kate had arranged to go straight to her new job, and her mother would follow within the week, after seeing their furniture put into store and returning the cottage key to its owner.

The owner of the village store had turned up trumps with an offer to drive Mrs Crosby to her new home with most of the luggage and Moggerty, so that Kate needed only her overnight bag and a case.

It was all very satisfactory, although her remaining days with Lady Cowder were uneasy, partly because Claudia had arrived unexpectedly, bringing with her the woman who was to replace Kate. She was a thin, sour-faced person with a sharp nose and grey hair scraped back into a bun. She followed Kate round the house on a tour of inspection, answering Kate's helpful remarks with sniffs of disapproval.

'I'll not have that cat in my kitchen,' she told Kate. 'The gardener can take it away and drown it.'

'No need,' said Kate, swallowing rage. 'Horace is coming with me, and may I remind you that until I leave I am still the housekeeper here.'

Miss Brown drew herself up with tremendous dignity, then said, 'I am sure I have no wish to interfere. It is to be hoped that your hoity-toity ways don't spoil your chances of earning a living.'

With which parting shot she took herself off to complain to Claudia, who in turn complained to Lady Cowder. That lady, who was guiltily aware that she had treated Kate badly, told her god-daughter with unexpected sharpness to tell Miss Brown to be civil and not interfere with Kate.

'Kate has been quite satisfactory while she has been with me, my dear, and she will be going to another job in two days' time.'

The next morning when Kate took up Lady Cowder's breakfast tray she waited until that lady had arranged herself comfortably against her pillows before saying quietly, 'Miss Brown doesn't want Horace in the house, Lady Cowder. May I take him with me?'

'The kitchen cat? I suppose so, if he'll go with you. Can he not be given to the gardener or someone? They'll know what to do with him.'

'They'll drown him.'

Lady Cowder gave a shudder. 'Really, Kate, must you tell me these unpleasant things just as I am about to have breakfast?'

When Kate said nothing and just stood there, Lady Cowder said pettishly, 'Oh, take the cat by all means. It is most unfair of you to cause this unpleasantness, Kate. It is perhaps a good thing that you are leaving my employ.'

She wasn't an unkind woman, although she was selfish and self-indulgent and lazy, so she added, 'Take the cat to your home this afternoon. Miss Brown can get our tea.'

Kate said, 'Thank you, Lady Cowder,' and went back to the kitchen to tell Horace that he would shortly have a new home. 'Where you will be loved,' she told him cheerfully, so that he lost the harassed expression he had had on his whiskery face ever since he had encountered Miss Brown.

Kate took him home later and, being an intelligent beast, knowing upon which side his bread was buttered, he made cautious overtures to Moggerty, explored the garden without attempting to leave it and settled down in the kitchen.

'Nice company for Moggerty,' observed Mrs Crosby.

Two days later Kate left Lady Cowder's house. It was still early morning, and Lady Cowder had bidden her goodbye on the previous evening. She had given Kate an extra week's salary, too, at the same time pointing out that her generosity was due to her kind nature.

'My god-daughter told me that I am being unnecessarily generous,' she pointed out to Kate. 'But as you will no doubt agree, I have been most liberal in my treatment of you, Kate.'

Kate would have liked to have handed the money back, only she couldn't afford to. Lady Cowder, waiting for grateful thanks and assurances of her generosity, frowned at Kate's polite thanks.

'Really,' she told Claudia later. 'Kate showed a lack of gratitude which quite shocked me.'

'Well, I told you so, didn't I? Brown wants to know at what time she should serve lunch...and I must go back home this afternoon.' She added carelessly, 'Have you heard anything of James lately?'

Lady Cowder looked thoughtful. 'No, I have been seeing quite a lot of him during the last month or so, but not recently. He's in great demand and probably working hard.'

*   *   *

Mr Tait-Bouverie was indeed working hard, but he still found time to think about Kate. He was aware that he could have made things much easier for Kate and her mother by driving them to their new home himself, but he had kept away. His Kate, he reflected ruefully, was suspicious of any help which smacked even slightly of charity. Besides, she was quite capable of putting two and two together and making five…

He would have to wait until she was settled in before paying a visit, so he took on even more work and at the weekends, if he happened to be free, went down to Bosham with Prince and spent the day sailing. He had a dear little cottage there; Kate would like it, and he would teach her to sail.

He came home late one evening after a long day at the hospital, and Mudd, meeting him in the hall, observed gravely that in his opinion Mr Tait-Bouverie was over-doing it.

'With all due respect, sir,' said Mudd, 'You are wearing yourself out; you need a wife.'

Mr Tait-Bouverie picked up his case and made for his study. 'Mudd, you're quite right. Will it make you happy if I tell you that I intend to take a wife?'

Mudd beamed. 'Really, sir? When will that be?'

'As soon as she'll have me, Mudd.'

Kate, getting ready for bed in Mrs Willett's cottage, presently laid her tired head on the pillow. It had been a crowded day; not least of all her arrival, her rather solemn reception by Mr Tombs followed by a brief five minutes with Mrs Braithewaite and then tea with the rest of the staff and finally going to bed in the cottage.

Mrs Willett had left that very afternoon to go straight to the hospital, leaving everything very neat and tidy, and all Kate had to do was go to bed, close her eyes and sleep until her alarm clock went off at half past six the following morning. But despite her tiredness, she allowed her thoughts to stray towards Mr Tait-Bouverie. She wondered sleepily what he was doing and wished that she could see him again.

'You are more than foolish,' said Kate loudly to herself, 'you are downright silly. Forget him.'

So she went to sleep and dreamed of him.

During the next day, and those following it, Kate made several discoveries. Mrs Braithewaite was old and crotchety, and she expected perfection, but she never failed to thank those who worked for her. Kate, used to Lady Cowder's demands, was thankful for that. The rest of the staff, even Mr Tombs, were friendly, anxious to put her at her ease and show her where everything was kept. Mr Tombs expressed the wish that she would find her stay with them a happy one, and that she was to consult him if any problem should arise.

As to her work, she was kept busy enough running the house, being careful not to upset Daisy or Meg or the two cleaning ladies who came each day—and besides that she had the stores to order, menus to discuss with Mrs Braithewaite and the cooking to do. She was free each afternoon for a couple of hours and free, too, once dinner had been served to Mrs Braithewaite and the rest of the staff had had their supper.

Her mother had followed her within a few days and the little cottage, decorated with a few of their personal ornaments and photographs, had taken on the aspect of home. Up early in the mornings, feeding Horace and Moggerty, taking tea to her mother and drinking her own by the open door leading to the little garden beyond the cottage, Kate was happy. It wasn't going to last; she knew that. But while it did she was content.

Well, almost content. Despite her best efforts, she found her thoughts wandering far too often towards Mr Tait-Bouverie. She hadn't expected to hear from him again, but all the same she was disappointed. Unable to forget the matter, she asked her mother, one day, in what she hoped was a casual manner if she thought he might find the time to phone them. 'Just to see if we've settled in,' Kate explained.

'Most unlikely,' her mother had said firmly. 'A busy man like him. After all, he has done all he could for us but that doesn't mean to say that he has to be bothered with us. He helped us and that's that, Kate.'

Mrs Crosby glanced at Kate's face, unwilling to agree that she had been disappointed, too. She had thought, quite wrongly, it seemed, that Mr Tait-Bouverie had had more than a passing interest in Kate. Well, she had been wrong; he had done an act of kindness and that was that. She went on cheerfully, 'I've been looking in the local paper—he was quite right, there are several hotels advertising for cooks or housekeepers. You'll get a job easily enough when we leave here. I shan't like that, will you? You're happier here, aren't you, Kate?'

'Yes, Mother. It's a nice job and Mrs Braithewaite is rather an old dear. I know she's strict but she's not mean. Compared with Lady Cowder she eats like a bird, although Mr Tombs tells me that she entertains from time to time on a lavish scale.'

Kate and her mother had been there just over two weeks when Kate, going off duty for her afternoon break, walked out of the kitchen door and saw Mr Tait-Bouverie. He was sitting, very much at his ease, on the stone wall by the door but he got down and came to meet her. His, 'Hello, Kate,' was casual in the extreme, which had the immediate effect of damping down her delight at seeing him.

She bade him a good afternoon in a severe manner and started to walk across the wide cobbled-stone yard, and he fell into step beside her. 'Pleased to see me, Kate?'

Of course she was, but she wasn't going to say so. She didn't answer that but observed in her calm way, 'I dare say you have come to see Mrs Braithewaite—you did mention that you knew her.'

'Of course I know her; she's one of my aunts. Are you going to invite me to your cottage?'

Kate stood still. 'Certainly not, Mr Tait-Bouverie. You know as well as I do that it's not possible.'

'You mean old Tombs will take umbrage?' He loomed over her, too close for her peace of mind. 'He taught me to ride my first bike. I used to stay here when I was a small boy.'

Kate was momentarily diverted. 'Did he? Did he, really? How old were you?'

She remembered suddenly that she must remain aloof. Grateful and friendly, of course—but aloof... 'You will excuse me if I go? I have only an hour or so, but I have several things that I want to do.'

He nodded. 'Wash your hair, rinse out the smalls, bake a cake. Stop making excuses, Kate; I asked if you were glad to see me?'

She stood there, rather tired from her morning's work, her hair not as tidy as it might be. He studied the curling tendrils of hair which had escaped, and only with difficulty stopped himself from taking the pins out and letting the whole gleaming mass fall round her shoulders.

Kate had her eyes fixed on his waistcoat; that seemed

the safest place. She said quietly, 'Yes, I'm glad to see you, Mr Tait-Bouverie.'

'Good. Has our friendship advanced sufficiently for you to call me James?'

'No! I mean—that is, it wouldn't do.'

'It will do very well indeed when we're alone.'

'Very well,' said Kate. 'I'll tell Mother that I have seen you, we—she talks about you from time to time.'

'I've visited your mother. While you were slaving over a hot stove I was drinking coffee in the cottage with her.' He saw her look. 'When I come here I look up the entire household. Tombs would be upset if I didn't spend half an hour with him, and I like a word with Daisy and Meg, and old Briggs. We had a pleasant chat, your mother and I. She is full of plans for your future.'

Kate nodded. 'Yes. You were quite right—there are plenty of jobs in Bath. When I leave here we'll find something there. Just as soon as—as it's possible, we'll look for somewhere to live and I can start...'

'That is still what you have set your heart on doing, Kate?'

She said soberly, 'Yes. Then we shall have a life of our own, won't we?'

'What if a man should come along and sweep you off your feet and marry you?'

'I'd like that very much, but since it isn't likely to happen...'

'Will you promise me to tell me when it does?'

He spoke lightly and she smiled at him. 'All right, I do promise.' She added hesitantly, 'Lady Cowder told me that you are to be married.'

'Did she, indeed? She is, of course, quite right.' He held out a hand. 'I'm going to have a chat with Briggs. I'm glad that you are happy here, Kate. Goodbye.'

She offered her hand and wished that he would never let it go. But he did, and she said a quiet goodbye and went on her way to the cottage. He had said goodbye, she reflected. She wouldn't see him again and this was hardly the time to discover that she was in love with him.

Her mother was in the small garden behind the cottage, with Horace and Moggerty curled up together beside her.

'You're late, darling,' she said. And then, when she saw Kate's face, 'What's the matter?' she asked. 'Something has upset you?'

'I met Mr Tait-Bouverie as I left the house. He—he was wandering around talking to everyone. He said he'd been to see you.' Kate took a slow breath. 'He said goodbye.'

'Yes, dear. He's going back to town this afternoon. We had coffee together—what a nice man he is, and so interested in our plans. He's off to America in a couple of days. He certainly leads a busy life.'

Indeed he led a busy life, Kate agreed silently. A life in which there was no place for her. He would become more and more successful and marry Claudia, who would arrange his social life for him, and see that he met all the right people. She would be good at that, ignoring his work and having no interest in it. He would be unhappy... Kate sighed—such a deep sigh that her mother gave her a thoughtful look.

'You're happy here, Kate? I know it isn't for long, but if all goes well we should be able to start on our own before the winter. I intend to get a job—part-time—so that I can look after us both while you get your catering started.'

That roused Kate from her unhappy thoughts. 'No, Mother, you're not to go out to work. There'll be no need—we can manage on the money I'll borrow from the bank. With luck I'll get one or two regular customers—hotels in Bath and small cafés—and we'll manage.'

They would too, Kate reflected. She would make a success of her cooking and catering and she and her mother would live in comfort for the rest of their lives. She would also forget Mr Tait-Bouverie...

As it happened that wasn't difficult to do, for the following morning she was summoned to Mrs Braithewaite's sitting room. She had seen very little of her since she had arrived to work for her, but she hadn't expected to—Mr Tombs relayed his mistress's requirements from day to day, and only occasionally had Kate been bidden to the old lady's presence.

'Not the sack,' thought Kate aloud, assuming her calm housekeeper's face and tapping on the door.

The old lady was sitting by the window, guarded from draughts by numerous shawls and scarves. She said tetchily, 'Come in, do, Kate. I hope you have your notebook and pen with you. There is a great deal to discuss.'

Kate advanced into the room and stood where her employer could see her. She said, 'Good morning, madam,' and produced her notebook and pencil without comment. Presumably a special dinner...

'It is my birthday in two weeks' time,' said Mrs Braithewaite. 'I shall be eighty-three years old and I intend to celebrate the occasion. I shall give a buffet luncheon for—let me see—about sixty or seventy persons. I do not require you to cook those tiresome morsels on biscuits, and bits and pieces. You are to do ham on the bone, and a whole salmon, of course—two, perhaps? Cheese tartlets, a good round of cold beef, chicken... I expect you to embellish these and add anything else suitable. Sweets, of course, something which can be eaten elegantly without trouble—possibly ice cream, which you will make yourself. What have you to say to that?'

'May I add suitable accompaniments to the main dishes, madam? And may I make out a menu and let you decide if it suits you?'

'Do that. I want it this evening, mind. If you need extra help in the kitchen, say so. Tombs will see to that.'

Mrs Braithewaite was suddenly impatient. 'Go along, Kate, you must have work to do.'

Tombs was waiting for her in the kitchen. 'This is to be a great occasion,' he told her solemnly. 'Mrs Braithewaite has many relations and friends. You will let me know if you need help, Kate, and please come to me for advice if you should need it.' His tone implied that he was quite sure that she would.

Kate thanked him nicely, aware that he was doubtful as to her capabilities when it came to such an undertaking. She had no doubts herself. She went back to her work and that afternoon she went over to the cottage, told her mother and sat down to assemble a suitable menu.

She presented herself later in Mrs Braithewaite's sitting room and handed her a menu and two alternatives.

Mrs Braithewaite adjusted her lorgnettes. 'What is a toad-in-the-hole?' she wanted to know.

'A morsel of cooked sausage in a very small Yorkshire pudding. They can be eaten in the hand.'

The old lady grunted. 'The salads seem adequate. See that there is enough of everything, Kate. And desserts—sorbets, of course, ice creams, Charlotte Russe, jellied fruits, trifle... Very well, that should suffice. Send Tombs to me, if you please.'

So for the next two weeks Kate had more than enough to do, keeping her too busy to think about anything other than food. There was an enormous freezer in the kitchen, so she was able to prepare a great deal of food in advance, and, although Mrs Braithewaite had said nothing about it, she baked a cake—rich with dried fruit, sherry and the best butter. She had wisely consulted Mr Tombs about this, and he had given it his blessing. Indeed, the kitchen staff had been consulted as to its decoration, to be undertaken at the last minute.

Kate's days were full; it was only when she laid her tired head on the pillow that she allowed her thoughts to dwell on Mr Tait-Bouverie. She supposed that he would come to the luncheon if he was back in England, but she was hardly likely to see him. She was unlikely to stir out of her kitchen.

Tombs had assembled casual help from the village to do the waiting, and she would remain in the kitchen and make sure that the food was transported safely upstairs to the big drawing room where trestle tables were to be erected, suitably swathed in white damask and decorated with the flowers that the gardener was cherishing for just such an occasion.

Mr Tait-Bouverie was back in England. His aunt's invitation was waiting for him when he returned from a weekend at Bosham, where he had spent a good deal of time thinking of good reasons why he should go and see Kate. Now the reason was most conveniently there.

He accepted with alacrity and Mudd, removing the well-worn and quite unsuitable garments which Mr Tait-Bouverie delighted in wearing when he was at Bosham, reflected with satisfaction that such an occasion would make it necessary for his master to be clothed in the superfine suiting—exquisitely tailored—the pristine linen and one of the silk ties which Mudd found fitting for a man of Mr Tait-Bouverie's standing.

'Just for luncheon, sir?' he wanted to know. 'Will you be staying overnight?'

'No, no, Mudd. I'll drive back here during the afternoon. It's a Saturday, isn't it? I'll go down to Bosham and spend Sunday there.'

Mudd nodded gloomily. He would do his best with the unsuitable garments, but that was all they would ever be in his eyes. He asked hopefully, 'You will be wearing the grey suiting, sir?'

Mr Tait-Bouverie, thinking about Kate, nodded absently. 'I'll need to leave the house early tomorrow morning, Mudd. Breakfast at seven o'clock?'

Mudd, his feelings soothed by the prospect of sending his master well-dressed to his luncheon date, assured him that breakfast would be on the table at exactly seven o'clock.

'Dinner will be ready in half an hour, sir.'

'Good; I'll be in the garden with Prince.'

He wandered around with Prince, enjoying the twilight of the early autumn evening, allowing his thoughts to dwell on the satisfactory prospect of seeing Kate again. He would have to go carefully…she was a proud girl, and stubborn. His pleasant thoughts were interrupted by Mudd, coming to tell him that Lady Cowder was on the phone.

'Dear boy,' cooed his aunt, 'you're back in England. Tell me, are you going to your aunt's luncheon party? Her birthday—just imagine, eighty-three and giving a party. I have been invited, of course, although we scarcely know each other. I mean, she is on your father's side of the family, isn't she? Of course, I have accepted, and begged to bring dear Claudia with me. May we beg a lift from you? And if you would be kind enough to drive us back after the party…?'

Mr Tait-Bouverie was a truthful man, but sometimes a lie was necessary. Certainly it was now—to spend several hours in Claudia's company was something he had no wish to do.

'Impossible, I'm afraid,' he said briskly. 'I shall be going, but only if I can fit it in with my work. Surely Claudia can drive you there and back? That is, if she accepts the invitation. She will know no one there, I presume?'

'She knows you,' said Lady Cowder, and gave a little titter. When he didn't have anything to say to that, she added, 'Oh, well, I thought I might ask you; I forget how busy you are. I do hope that we will see you there and have time for a chat. Claudia is always talking about you.'

Mr Tait-Bouverie said, 'Indeed,' in a cold voice, and then, 'Forgive me if I ring off; Mudd has just put dinner on the table.'

'Oh, how thoughtless of me, James. Tell me, before you go, how is your dear mother?'

'In splendid health.' And when he had no more to add to that, Lady Cowder rang off herself.

He was eating his breakfast the next morning when his mother phoned. 'James, I do hope I haven't got you out of bed? I'm back...I know I'm not supposed to be here until tomorrow, but there was a seat on the plane and I thought I'd transfer. Can I come to your place and tidy up before I go home?'

'Mother, dear, stay just where you are—I'm on my way to work, but Mudd shall fetch you at once. You'll stay here as long as you like. I'll be home later today and Mudd will look after you. Did you leave everyone well in Toronto?'

'Splendid, dear. The baby's a darling. I'll tell you all the news when I see you.'

'Go and have breakfast or coffee, my dear; Mudd will be as quick as he can.'

He put down the phone and found Mudd at his elbow. 'Mrs Tait-Bouverie is back, Mudd. Will you take the Rover and fetch her from Heathrow? Take Prince with you…no, on second thoughts he had better stay at home. It's Mrs Todd's day for cleaning, isn't it? She'll keep an eye on him. Mother is sure to have a great deal of luggage.'

'Mrs Todd has already arrived, sir. I will inform her of what has happened and go immediately to the airport.'

Mudd spoke with his usual dignity, refusing to be hassled by the unexpected. Mr Tait-Bouverie swallowed his coffee and prepared to leave his house. 'Splendid, Mudd. And think up one of your dinners for this evening, will you?'

'I have already borne that in mind, sir,' said Mudd.

There was a hint of reproach in his voice, and Mr Tait-Bouverie said at once, 'You're a paragon, Mudd. I would be lost without you.'

Mudd, aware of his worth, merely inclined his head gravely.

Mrs Tait-Bouverie was sharing a sofa with Prince when her son got home that evening. He was tired; his outpatients clinic had been larger than usual, and he had interrupted his ward round in order to see a badly injured child brought into the accident room.

His mother offered a cheek for his kiss. 'You've had a long day, James.'

'Yes, Mother, but it's so nice to come home to you…'

'You should be coming home to your wife.'

He sat down opposite to her and picked up the glass

Mudd had put on the table beside his chair. 'Something I hope to do.'

Mrs Tait-Bouverie put down her glass of sherry. 'James, dear, you've found her...?'

'Yes.' He glanced at his mother—a tall woman, a little given to stoutness, but still good-looking, and with a charming smile. She dressed beautifully to please herself and was always elegant.

He went on, 'She has a lovely face, and quantities of russet hair. She is tall, as tall as you, and she has a delightful voice. She is cook-housekeeper to Aunt Edith Braithewaite.'

'Why?' asked his mother.

'Fallen on hard times after her father died. She lives with her mother.'

'Not one of those beanpole girls playing at earning her living?'

'No, no. She has no money.' He grinned suddenly. 'And she has what I believe are described as "generous curves".'

His mother accepted a second glass of sherry. 'She sounds exactly right for you. Has she agreed to marry you?'

'Certainly not. I imagine that she is unaware that I'm in love with her. Certainly she treats me with a cautious politeness, which is a bit disconcerting.'

'When shall I see her?'

'We are invited to Aunt Edith's birthday luncheon. She will be in the kitchen, of course. We must contrive a meeting.'

'When is this luncheon to be?'

'Ten days' time. Will you stay until then?'

'No, my dear. I'd like to go home and make sure that

everything is all right. Have you managed to go there at all?'

'Twice. It's too far for a day's drive; I managed weekends. Everything was all right. You could easily stay here, and I'll drive you up to Northumberland after the party.'

'I think I'd like to go home first. I'll get Peggy to drive me down. Did you see her while you were there?'

'Yes. She seems very happy. I'm to be an uncle again, I hear.'

'Yes. Isn't that splendid? Your sisters have given me several grandchildren, James. It's time you did the same.'

He smiled at her. 'All in good time, my dear. Here is Mudd to tell us that dinner is on the table.'

Two weeks wasn't long in which to plan and prepare the kind of luncheon Mrs Braithewaite insisted upon giving. Kate sat up late at night, writing copious notes and then assembling everything she would need. A good deal could be prepared well ahead of the day, but catering for seventy people was a challenge. Luckily the staff, led by a self-important Mr Tombs, were delighted with the idea of such a social gathering and went out of their way to help Kate—Tombs going so far as to drive her into Bath so that she could choose what she needed for herself and then stow it away in the huge freezer until she needed it.

All the same, even with so much willing help, there was a lot to do. Kate enjoyed it, though. Cooking for Lady Cowder had been a thankless task, but now, as she made tartlets and pork pies, cooked the hams to an exact pinkness, coated chicken breasts in a creamy cheese sauce, made lobster patties and crisp potato straws, she felt satisfaction.

On the day previous to the luncheon she stayed up until the small hours, making bowls of mouthwatering trifle, puréeing fruit to mix with gelatine and turn out into colourful shapes. And the cake... She had baked that days ago; now she iced it, decorated it with the roses she had fashioned so carefully and set a single candle amongst them.

Mr Tombs had advised that. 'Mrs Braithewaite hasn't enough breath to blow out one candle, let alone eighty-three,' he had told her seriously.

The great day dawned with a clear sky, although there was an autumnal nip in the air. Luncheon was to be served at one o'clock, and Kate and her helpers were up and about before the sun was up. The tables had to be set up, draped with damask, decorated with flowers and set with plates and cutlery, glass and napkins.

They ate a hasty breakfast and Kate assembled what she would need for dinner that evening. There were to be guests staying on—ten people, close family of Mrs Braithewaite—and she had been warned to send up a four-course meal. Rack of lamb with suitable accompaniments, a sorbet, Charlotte Russe and, for starters, mushrooms in a garlic and cream sauce. For the kitchen staff she had wisely made a vast steak and kidney pudding which could be cut into and kept warm if need be.

The guests began to arrive at around noon and Mr Tombs, Daisy and Meg went upstairs to take coats and hand around sherry. Kate, a little nervous now, put the finishing touches to the cake and put on a clean pinny. Now was her chance to nip up to the drawing room where the buffet had been arranged and make sure that everything was just as it should be.

She paused on the threshold and sighed with satisfaction. The tables were loaded with food but they looked elegant. The flowers were perfect and the hams on their

vast dishes, surrounded by dishes of various salads,
looked mouthwatering. The cake, of course, was to be
brought in at the end of luncheon, to be cut by Mrs
Braithewaite and handed round with champagne. Kate
nodded her bright head, well satisfied.

Mrs Tait-Bouverie, just that minute arrived and strolling
round the hall while James put the car away, paused
to look at her. Even from the back Mrs Tait-Bouverie
knew who she was. There weren't many heads of hair like
hers—besides, James had described her very accurately.
Mrs Tait-Bouverie wandered a little nearer, and when
Kate turned round to go she was pleased to see that he
had been quite right about Kate's looks, too. A beautiful
creature and plenty of her, thought his mother. She said
pleasantly, 'May I take a peep, or is it to be a surprise at
one o'clock?'

Kate smiled at her. 'Well, yes, I suppose it should be.
Mr Tombs said that no one was to go into the room until
then. I'm the cook, and I came to make sure everything
was as it should be.'

Mrs Tait-Bouverie surveyed the colourful display. 'It
looks magnificent. Caterers, I suppose?'

'Well, no,' said Kate matter-of-factly. 'It's all been
done here. We all helped.'

'But who did the cooking?'

'I did—only I couldn't have done it without everyone's
help. I'd better go—and if you don't mind I'll shut the
door...'

Which she did, and with a polite murmur went back to
the kitchen. Mrs Tait-Bouverie strolled back to the entrance
to meet her son.

'I've been talking to your Kate,' she told him. 'She's
everything you said of her, my dear, and I suspect a lot

more besides. She had no idea who I was. You'll go and find her before we leave?'

'Yes. There should be plenty of opportunity. The house is packed with people; we had better join them.'

CHAPTER EIGHT

MR TAIT-BOUVERIE following his mother, entered the smaller drawing room, where his aunt was sitting receiving her guests. A slow business, as she insisted on opening each present as it was offered to her. She greeted Mrs Tait-Bouverie with a peck on the cheek and turned to James.

'So you found the time to come?' she observed, and added slyly, 'Your Aunt Cowder is here with that girl...wanted to know where you were.'

He bent to kiss her cheek and she added wistfully, 'I should like to see you married, my dear.' She chuckled. 'Not to Claudia, of course.'

He said, 'Since it's your birthday, I believe it very likely that you will have your wish granted.'

He offered his gift, suitably wrapped and beribboned, and, leaving his mother with the old lady, wandered off to greet family and friends.

It wasn't long before Lady Cowder saw him.

'James, how delightful. You managed to get here, after all.' She pecked his cheek and added archly, 'Claudia is so looking forward to seeing you.'

Claudia, James saw at a glance, was dressed to kill— her make-up had been applied by a skilled hand and her blonde hair had been arranged in a fashionable tangle which, while in the forefront of the current mode, did nothing for her... Mr Tait-Bouverie shook hands, said ev-

erything necessary for good manners, and excused himself, giving his aunt a vague reply when she wanted to
know when he would be returning.

'Of course, he knows everyone here,' said Lady
Cowder soothingly to Claudia, and wished uneasily that
the girl would at least disguise her peevishness with a
smile.

The last of the guests having arrived, drinks were
handed round, a toast was drunk to their hostess and
Tombs announced that luncheon was being served from
the buffet.

This was a signal for a well-mannered rush to fill plates
while Tombs carved the hams and Daisy and Meg and
the girls pressed into service from the village saw to it
that everyone was served.

When that was done everyone settled down to eating
and gossip, having their plates replenished from time to
time and drinking the excellent wines Mrs Braithewaite
had provided. That lady was seated in some state at a table
at one end of the room while an ever-changing stream of
people came and went to exchange a few words with her.
Everyone was, in fact, fully occupied, and Mr Tait-
Bouverie had no difficulty in slipping away unseen.

The house was quiet once he had left the drawing room,
gone down the staircase and through the baize door at the
back of the hall to the kitchen. He opened its door quietly
and paused to enjoy the sight of Kate, fast asleep in one
of the shabby armchairs by the Aga.

She had kicked off her shoes and slept like a child, her
mouth slightly open, confident that she had the place to
herself for an hour or more. The last of the food had been
carried upstairs and there was nothing for her to do until
Tombs came to tell her to make the tea which some of

the guests, at least, would undoubtedly want. So she slept
dreamlessly, aware of a job well done.

Mr Tait-Bouverie trod silently across the kitchen and
sat down in the equally shabby chair opposite her, quite
happy to wait. He had dismissed a strong wish to kiss
Kate awake, and contented himself with watching her
tired, sleeping face.

Presently she opened her eyes, stared at him unbeliev-
ingly for a moment and, Kate being Kate, asked, 'Was I
snoring?'

Mr Tait-Bouverie stayed where he was. 'No,' he said
placidly. 'What time did you get up this morning, Kate?'

'Me? Four o'clock—I had to finish icing the cake. How
did you get here?'

'I came down the stairs. Shall I make us a pot of tea?'

'That would be lovely…' She stopped and sat up
straight. 'I'm sorry, Mr Tait-Bouverie, did you come with
a message, or want something? I'm sorry I fell asleep.'

He perceived that any rash ideas he might have had
about asking her to marry him would have to be ignored
for the moment. A pity, for he saw her so seldom, and
now, with plenty of time in which to tell her of his feelings, he would have to waste it making tea. He smiled at
the thought.

'No, no, everything is going splendidly upstairs. I came
to see if you were still quite happy here.'

He got up, opened up the Aga and put the kettle on,
found a teapot and the tea and two mugs, whistling quietly
as he did so—a sound which Kate found reassuring and
in some strange way comforting.

'A very successful birthday party,' said Mr Tait-
Bouverie. 'Have you had lunch?' And when she said that
she had not, he asked, 'Breakfast?'

'Well, I didn't have any time…'

'As a small boy,' said Mr Tait-Bouverie in a voice so soothing it would have reduced a roaring lion to tears, 'I was taught to boil an egg, make toast and butter it—my mother being of the opinion that if I could master these arts I would never starve.'

He had found the bread and the eggs and was busy at the Aga. 'Is your mother well? I must go over to the cottage and see her before we leave.'

Kate's tired brain fastened on the 'we'. 'Oh, you came with Claudia, I expect.'

The fragrant smell of toast made her twitch her pretty nose, and she didn't see his quick glance.

'No. I came with my mother. She's back from Canada, and came down from Northumberland. She and Aunt Edith are close friends.'

He placed a plate of well-buttered toast on the table and dished up an egg. 'Come and eat something.' When she had sat down at the table he poured the tea, a strong brew capable of reviving anyone not actually dead.

Kate ate her egg, polished off the toast and, imbued with new energy by the tea, got to her feet.

'That was lovely, thank you very much. I mustn't keep you, Mr Tait-Bouverie.' She popped a crumb into her mouth. 'I'm very grateful, but I mustn't keep you. It was most kind…' She stopped herself saying it all again.

She didn't quite look at him, and it was an effort to remember that she was the cook and must behave accordingly.

He made no attempt to leave. 'You have made your plans for the future?' he wanted to know. 'I am told that Mrs Willett will be returning in another few weeks, but I'm sure you will find something in Bath until you are ready to start on your own.'

'Yes. I shall start looking round in a week or two. Bath

seems a very pleasant place. Mother has been there—to look round, you know. I'm sure I'll find something.'

They were standing facing each other and she said again, 'Don't let me keep you—you're missing the party.'

When he didn't move, she added, 'It's a success, I hope? Mrs Braithewaite was so anxious that it should go off well. I hope she had some lovely presents—it's quite an achievement to be eighty-three and still have so many friends to wish one well…'

She spoke in her cook's voice, saying anything which came into her head, because if she didn't she might fling herself at him and pour out all her hopes and fears and love for him. She added, 'I must start the clearing up…'

'Of course. I'm glad you are happy here, Kate. I must go back upstairs and have a word with friends I haven't seen for some time.'

She nodded and answered his goodbye in a voice as cheerful as his own. It was pure chance which had caused them to meet again, she told herself when he had gone, and chances like that seldom happened twice.

Claudia was there, upstairs in the drawing room, looking, according to Daisy, quite lovely. Kate began to stack dishes, put away uneaten food and set out cups and saucers for the tea that the staff would undoubtedly be wanting later.

As for Mr Tait-Bouverie, he crossed the courtyard behind the house and paid a visit to her mother.

She greeted him warmly. 'Is it any good offering you coffee?' she asked. 'I expect you've had it already. Is the party a success?'

'Indeed, it is. A magnificent banquet; Kate can be proud of herself.'

'It was hard work,' Mrs Crosby said eagerly. 'But you

see, James, that she could make a career out of her cooking, once she can get started?'

'If that is indeed what she wants.' He took the mug of coffee she offered him. 'Mrs Crosby—you're tired, or not feeling well…'

She said far too quickly, 'I'm fine.' And then, catching his eyes, 'Well, it's just this silly little pain; it comes and goes. Even when it's not there I know that it is, if you see what I mean.' She smiled. 'It's nothing; really, it isn't…'

'Does Kate know?'

'No, of course not. She has had enough to think about for the last two weeks—up at dawn and going to bed at all hours. I'll go and see a doctor when the festivities are over.'

'This pain,' said Mr Tait-Bouverie. 'Tell me where it is, Mrs Crosby.'

She told him, because suddenly he wasn't James but a kind, impersonal doctor asking her questions in a quiet voice.

'I would not wish to alarm you, Mrs Crosby,' he told her. 'But I think that you should go to a doctor and allow him to examine you.' He smiled suddenly. 'Nothing serious, I do assure you, but from what you tell me I should suspect a grumbling appendix, which nowadays can be dealt with in a few days. Do you have a doctor?'

'No. I expect I can find one in Bath.'

'Allow me to arrange a check-up for you—I've a colleague in Bath who will see you. I'll phone him this evening and let you know when he can see you.'

'If it's necessary. I don't want Kate worried.' She added, 'You're very kind. You help us so often.'

'I'll let Kate know and reassure her.' He put down his mug. 'I must go back to the party.' He stood up and took her hand. 'Mrs Crosby, if you or Kate need help will you let me know? Phone my house. Even if I'm not there, my man will see that I get your message.'

He loosed her hand, scribbled in his pocket book and took out the page. 'Here is the number.'

Mr Tait-Bouverie wasn't a man to waste time. At home that evening he phoned his colleague in Bath, made an appointment for Mrs Crosby and picked up the phone to tell Kate.

She was making a last round of the kitchen, making sure that everything was ready for the morning. Daisy and Meg had already gone to their beds and the helpers from the village had long since gone. Mr Tombs had bidden her goodnight, expressed himself satisfied with her efforts and gone upstairs to check windows and doors and lock up. He had looked at her pale face and said kindly, 'You did a good job, Kate. Mrs Braithewaite was pleased.'

Kate was on the point of leaving the kitchen when the phone rang. She went to answer it, wondering who it could be, for it was used almost solely to order groceries and receive calls from tradespeople. Mr Tait-Bouverie's voice, very calm in her ear, took her by surprise so that she had no breath for a moment. When he said her name for a second time she said, 'Yes, it's me.'

'You're tired, but this is most important. I went to see your mother this afternoon. I'm not sure, but from what she tells me she may have a threatening appendicitis. Nothing to worry about, provided it's nipped in the bud. I've arranged for a Dr Bright in Bath to see your mother on Monday afternoon. He'll examine her, and if he thinks it's necessary he'll have her in hospital and take her appendix out. It's a simple operation and she will be quite fit in a few weeks.'

He was silent, and Kate said angrily, 'Why wasn't I told? How ill is Mother? I had no idea, and now you're telling me all this just as though it's not important, as though she's got a cold in the head or cut her hand...'

'Forgive me, Kate. You are always so sensible and practical, and I thought that I could tell you without wrapping it up in soft talk and caution.'

'Well, you're wrong. I've got feelings like everyone else—except you, of course. I don't suppose you feel anything except pleasure in nailing bones together and dancing with Claudia. You don't know about loving...' She gave a great sniff and hung up, then snatched up the phone again, appalled at what she had just said. 'No, no. I don't mean a word of it...'

The line was dead, of course.

To find a quiet corner and have a good cry was out of the question; Kate locked the door behind her and went to the cottage. Her mother gave her a guilty look as she went in and Kate said at once, 'Mr Tait-Bouverie has just been phoning me, Mother.' She spoke cheerfully and managed a smile, too. 'I had no idea that you weren't feeling well—I should have seen for myself...'

'Darling, you had more than enough to think about. Besides, I'm not really ill. What did James say?'

Kate told her. 'I expect there'll be a letter in the post on Monday morning. I'll ask Mrs Braithewaite if I can have the afternoon off and we'll catch the bus in after lunch. A Dr Bright is going to see you, and if he thinks he should he'll refer you to the hospital. We can't make any plans for the moment until we know what's to happen.'

Kate put her arms round her mother. 'I'm sorry, Mother, dear—it was very brave of you not to say something.'

'This birthday party was important, Kate. Once you start on your own you may find it useful; a lot of the guests are local people, and news gets around in the country.'

'None of that matters while you're not well, mother. I'm going to make us a warm drink and you're going to bed. We'll know more on Monday.'

There was a letter on Monday morning, giving the time and the place where Mrs Crosby was to go and, what was more, Tombs himself took Kate aside after breakfast and informed her that Mrs Braithewaite, having been appraised of Mrs Crosby's indisposition, had ordered Mr Briggs to drive them both to Bath and bring them back.

Kate stared at him, her eyes wide. 'Mr Tombs, however did Mrs Braithewaite know? I've certainly not told her—I intended to do so this morning...'

'As to that, Kate, I am quite unable to say,' he told her severely, mindful of Mr James's express wish that the source of the arrangement should be kept secret.

'I've talked to my aunt, Tombs,' Mr Tait-Bouverie had continued. 'And she has agreed to sending Briggs with the car, so not a word to a soul.'

Tombs had assured him that he would be as quiet as the grave.

So Kate and her mother were driven in comfort to see Dr Bright, a youngish man, who examined Mrs Crosby and then told her in his pleasant voice that she should go into hospital as soon as possible and have her appendix out.

'Which hospital?' asked Kate. 'You see, we don't actually live here...'

'Ah—as to that, I think things could be arranged. You are acquainted with Mr Tait-Bouverie, are you not? He is an old friend and colleague of mine—and an honorary consultant at our hospital; there should be no trouble in finding a bed for you for a week or ten days—and you are an emergency, Mrs Crosby. I should like you to come tomorrow and be seen by the surgeon there—also a colleague of Mr Tait-Bouverie—and he will decide when he will operate. The sooner the better. The operation is simple, but nonetheless necessary.'

When Mrs Crosby hesitated, Kate said, 'You are very kind, Doctor. If you will tell me where Mother has to go and at what time…?'

'Would you wait while I arrange a bed?' said Dr Bright, and ushered them back into the waiting room, to emerge in ten minutes or so.

'Bring Mrs Crosby to the hospital at two o'clock tomorrow afternoon. She will be seen then, and admitted.'

He shook hands with them both, said that he would be seeing Mrs Crosby again very shortly, and went back to his surgery and lifted the phone.

Kate was surprised at the amount of willing help she was offered when she told Mr Tombs the result of their visit to the doctor. She had expected him to grumble, even make it difficult for her to go with her mother to the hospital the next day, but he had been helpful. She was to go with her mother directly after lunch and stay until she was quite satisfied that Mrs Crosby was comfortable, and she had seen the surgeon.

'But dinner,' said Kate. 'I may not be back in time to cook it.'

'You have the morning,' Mr Tombs reminded her. 'Prepare a dish which Daisy or Meg can warm up. They are quite capable of cooking the vegetables. Unless Mrs Braithewaite asks for a special dessert, you will have time in the morning to make a trifle. She is partial to trifle.'

Kate thanked him and started to cook that evening's dinner, and make a steak and kidney pie for the staff supper. She made two; one would do for the next day. She had seen her mother safely back to the cottage and left her to pack a case and get ready for the next day. She hated leaving her alone, but Mrs Braithewaite had been kind so far, and so had Mr Tombs, but she was still the cook with a job to do.

Briggs took them to Bath the following day. Tombs had taken Kate aside while she was getting the breakfast and told her that Mrs Braithewaite had herself suggested it. 'And when you are ready to return, she wishes you to telephone to me and I will instruct Briggs to fetch you from the hospital,' said Tombs at his most pompous.

It was a surprise, too, when Mrs Crosby was taken to a small room opening out of the women's surgical ward. Kate said anxiously to the sister, 'Is there some mistake? I mean, Mother's on the NHS—we can't afford to pay— and this is a private room, isn't it?'

Sister smiled. 'It is the only bed we have free,' she explained. 'And of course you won't have to pay for it. Your mother will be here for a week or ten days at the most. Is there someone to look after her when she goes home?'

'Me,' said Kate. 'I'm a cook; we have a little cottage close to the house. I can manage quite well as long as Mother can be left while I work.'

'It should be perfectly all right.' Sister patted Kate's arm. 'You mustn't worry; I'm sure Dr Bright told you that it is a simple operation, and only needs a short stay in hospital. I'll leave you to get your mother settled in and then, if you will come to my office, I dare say Mr Samuels will see you. He's the surgeon who will operate.'

He was quite a young man, Kate discovered, and he told her that he would operate on the following day. Possibly in the afternoon. 'I'll get someone to let you know, then if you wish to see your mother you will be able to do so.'

'I'm not sure if I can get away. You see, I'm a cook and there's dinner to prepare. I've been given a lot of free time already...' Kate added anxiously, 'If I phoned, would someone tell me if everything was all right? I'll come if I possibly can...'

'Don't worry if you can't come,' he assured her. 'We'll keep you informed, and I'm sure Sister will let you visit whenever you can manage it.'

So Kate bade a cheerful goodbye to her mother and phoned Mr Tombs, who told her to wait at the hospital entrance until Briggs came to fetch her. 'I trust everything is satisfactory, Kate?' he added.

Kate said that, yes, it was, and thanked him once again. 'Everyone is being so helpful,' she told him.

Mr Tait-Bouverie would have been pleased to hear that. He had spent time and thought and hours on the phone, persuading and explaining, shamelessly taking advantage of his consultant's post at the hospital. Because he was well liked by his colleagues—and Tombs hid a lifelong devotion to him—he had succeeded in his plan. Only Mrs Braithewaite had demanded to know why he should be taking so much trouble over her cook's mother.

'I'm sure Kate's mother is a very pleasant person,' she had stated. 'But, after all, Kate is the cook, James.'

'She is my future wife.' Mr Tait-Bouverie heard the old lady gasp. 'So, dear Aunt Edith, will you do as I ask?'

'Does she know?'

'No.'

Mrs Braithewaite chuckled. 'She is an excellent cook and a very pretty girl, and it's time you settled down. Come and see me when you have the time, James; I dare say you have some scheme in that clever head of yours.'

'Indeed, I have. And I'm free tomorrow.'

'I shall expect you!'

The operation was a success. Kate was called to answer the phone just as she had sent Mrs Braithewaite's lunch up on Daisy's tray. Sister was reassuringly cheerful. 'Your mother is back in bed and sleeping peacefully.'

'I thought it was to be this afternoon.' Kate did her best to keep the wobble out of her voice; it was silly to want to cry now that everything was all right.

'Mr Samuels decided to do your mother at the end of his morning list.' Sister had hesitated before she spoke, but Kate was in no state to notice.

'Please give Mother my love when she wakes up, and I'll come when I can. Would this evening be too late?'

'Come when you can,' said Sister comfortably. 'Your mother will probably be asleep, but if you visit her you'll feel better, won't you?'

Kate put down the phone. She was crying, although she had tried her best not to. Everything was all right, Sister had said, but she longed to be with her mother—just for a minute or two. Just to make quite sure...

Mr Tombs came to a silent halt beside her, and she blew her nose and sniffed back the tears. 'That was the hospital, Mr Tombs. Mother is back in her bed and everything is fine. Sister said so.'

'We are all relieved at the good news,' said Tombs, looking suitably serious. 'I will inform Mrs Braithewaite and I suggest that you go and have your dinner with the rest of the staff, Kate.'

He went on his dignified way and Kate went back to the kitchen, to be cheered by the kind enquiries she had from Daisy and Meg and the daily woman from the village. She couldn't eat her dinner, and only drank the strong tea Daisy gave her, her head filled with rather wild plans to go to Bath and see her mother. This evening, she reflected, once dinner had been served, she would get a taxi. No one would object to that, and she would be back before Tombs locked up for the night.

She got up and went along to the fridge; preparations for dinner needed to be made and Mrs Braithewaite wanted scones for her tea.

Tombs came looking for her. 'I have informed Mrs Braithewaite of your mother's operation, Kate. I am to tell Briggs to drive you to the hospital at half past seven this evening.'

Kate put down the dish of Dover sole she was inspecting. 'He will? I may go with him? How very kind of Mrs Braithewaite. I was going to ask you if it would be all right for me to get a taxi once dinner had been served, Mr Tombs.'

She smiled, wanting to cry from sheer relief. 'I'll have everything quite ready if Daisy or Meg won't mind dishing up.'

'They are glad to help you, Kate. If you wish to telephone the hospital you have my permission to do so.'

There wasn't much time once Kate had cooked dinner, so she hurried over to the cottage, tore into a jumper and skirt and shabby jacket, tied a scarf over her hair and, anxious not to keep Briggs waiting, went quickly to the other side of the yard where he would be ready.

'Sorry I'm late, Mr Briggs,' she told him breathlessly. 'It's been a bit of a rush.'

'Just you sit and catch your breath, Kate. It's a nasty

old night—going to rain; chilly, too. Your ma's in the best place, I reckon.'

Certainly, Kate thought as she got out at the hospital entrance, it looked cheerful, with lights shining from every window. She paused to poke her head through the car window. 'I'll not be long, Mr Briggs. Will you be here, or shall I meet you somewhere? The car park?'

'You come here, Kate.'

He drove away when she had gone inside.

Kate went to the reception desk and waited impatiently while the girl phoned the ward. She was to go up, she was told. She could take the lift, or the stairs were at the back of the hall.

She raced up the stairs two at a time and then paused to calm down before she pushed open the ward doors. A nurse came to meet her and led her through the ward and into the short corridor onto which her mother's room opened.

'Your mother's fine, but tired,' said the nurse, and smiled and left her.

Mrs Crosby, comfortably propped up with pillows, was rather pale but almost her usual cheerful self. She said happily, 'Kate, dear, how lovely. How did you get here?'

'Briggs brought me, Mother. How lovely to have it all over and done with. Are you comfortable? Does it hurt? Are you being well looked after?'

'I'm being treated like a film star, and I'm only a bit sore. I'm to get out of bed tomorrow.'

Kate embraced her parent rather gingerly, and pulled up a chair.

'So soon? Do you want anything? I'm not sure if I can come tomorrow, but I'll be here on Friday—it's my day off, and I can get the bus. Do you want any more nighties?

What about books? Fruit? I couldn't bring flowers; there wasn't a shop open.'

She took her mother's hand in hers. 'Mother, dear, I'm so glad that they discovered your appendix before it got too bad. I'll ask if I can see the surgeon and thank him.'

'Yes, dear, such a nice man. But it's James we have to thank. He knew what to do.'

'Yes, yes, of course. I'll write and thank him, shall I?'

She remembered what she had said to him on the phone and blushed hotly. It would be a difficult letter to write. And it would serve her right if he tore it up without reading it.

She didn't stay long; her mother was already half-asleep. She bent and kissed her, and went back down the ward and tapped on Sister's office door.

Sister was there, sitting at her desk, and so was Mr Samuels. Mr Tait-Bouverie was there too, lounging against the windowsill.

Kate stopped short in the doorway. She said 'Oh,' uncertainly and then, 'I'm sorry—I didn't know…'

'Come in, Miss Crosby,' said Sister briskly. 'You've visited your mother?' When Kate nodded, she added, 'Well, since Mr Samuels is here I expect he'll tell you that everything is just as it should be.'

Kate transferred her eyes to his face, careful not to look at Mr Tait-Bouverie after that first startled glance.

'Your mother is doing well. Nothing to worry about. A nasty appendix; we caught it just in time. She'll be up and about in no time.' He smiled nicely. 'Of course, you know Mr Tait-Bouverie, don't you? Lucky he got the ball rolling, so to speak.'

Kate cast a look at Mr Tait-Bouverie's waistcoat. 'Yes, I'm very grateful. Thank you very much, Mr Samuels.

And Sister. I'm being taken back—someone's waiting for me—I'd better go. I'll come again as soon as I can.'

Mr Tait-Bouverie hadn't uttered a word. Now he said quietly, 'I'll drive you back, Kate.'

'No.' Kate spoke loudly and too quickly before she could stop herself. She felt her face grow hot. 'What I mean is,' she added lamely, 'Mr Briggs is waiting for me.'

'He went straight back to my aunt's house. If you're ready?'

He stood up and went to the door, and she saw that there was nothing else to do but go with him. Mr Samuels was smiling, and so was Sister...

She thanked them both once more, shook hands and went past Mr Tait-Bouverie, who was holding the door open for her.

Halfway down the stairs she stopped. 'You arranged everything, didn't you. Mother being operated upon so quickly, having a private room, Briggs driving us to and fro...'

'Yes.' He had stopped beside her, his face impassive.

'I didn't mean a word of it,' she burst out. 'All that about you not having any feelings. I—I was taken by surprise and frightened for Mother, but that's no excuse.' She took a couple of steps down. 'You don't have to take me back; I feel awful.' She stopped again and added fiercely, 'You must know how I feel, calling you all those awful things, and you still helped Mother. If you never want to speak to me again I'd quite understand.'

He said placidly, 'What a silly girl you are, Kate.' He made it sound like an endearment. 'True, I have satisfaction—not pleasure—in nailing bones together, as you put it. And I do enjoy dancing—but not with Claudia. And, contrary to your opinion of me, I do know how to love.'

They had reached the bottom of the staircase. Kate's

tongue ran away with her. 'If you're going to marry Claudia you ought to enjoy dancing with her,' she said foolishly.

'Why, yes, I suppose I should,' he agreed. 'Now come along; the car is round in the consultants' car park.'

She went with him, silent now. He had called her a silly girl and she supposed that she was—and if that was what he thought of her, she had indeed been silly to fall in love with him. She got into the car and answered his casual observations about her mother in a stiff little voice.

At the house he got out of the car with her, walked her to the kitchen door, opened it, bade her a cheerful goodnight and waited until she had gone inside before walking to the front door.

Tombs, on the look-out for the car, was waiting to open it for him. Mr Tait-Bouverie greeted him with a gentle thump on the back. 'I have just returned Kate to the kitchen,' he told him. 'Mrs Crosby is doing very well. Is my aunt in the drawing room?'

'Yes, Mr James, and there's coffee and sandwiches. You're no doubt hungry...'

Mrs Braithewaite was sitting by the fire, swathed in a shawl and with her feet on a stool. She looked decidedly elderly sitting there, but there was nothing elderly about her voice.

'Come in, James. I must say, this is a fine time of day to call on me. I should be in bed...'

He bent and kissed her cheek. 'Aunt Edith, you know, and so do I, that you're never in bed before midnight.'

'An old woman of my age...' she began, and then went on, 'Oh, well since I'm here...pour yourself a whisky and you can give me one, too...'

He poured a small drink for her, added ice and gave

himself a more generous drink. 'You shouldn't be drinking spirits at your age,' he told her mildly.

'At my age I'll drink anything I like!' she told him.
'Sit down; where's Kate?'

'I would suppose that she has gone to her home.'

His aunt chuckled. 'Was she surprised to see you? Did
you sweep her off her feet?'

'Oh, she was surprised. But it hardly seemed the right
moment to behave with anything but the utmost circumspection.'

'Oh, well, I suppose you know best. How's your
mother?'

'Very well. Aunt Edith, when is Mrs Willett returning?'

'Hah! I might have known you had some scheme up
your sleeve. In two weeks; it seems she has made great
progress. She will come back here, of course, and your
Kate will have to go.'

'Splendid. It will be too far to take Mrs Crosby up to
Mother's. I intend to offer her the cottage at Bosham.
When Kate leaves here, she will join her there...'

'Will she? She might not want to, James. Aren't you
taking a lot for granted?'

'Possibly. It's a calculated risk, isn't it? But she will
have nowhere else to go.'

'You're a prize catch, James—good looks, money, well
liked, well known in your profession, comfortable ances-
tral home, even if it is in the north, fashionable house in
town, cottage at Bosham. I'm surprised that Kate hasn't
flung herself into your arms.'

'Kate doesn't care tuppence for any of that,' said Mr
Tait-Bouverie. 'She's proud—the right kind of pride—and
she's in love with me and won't admit it because she has
this bee in her bonnet about Claudia, Lady Cowder's god-
daughter. She has this idea that I'm on the point of mar-

rying the girl. The last thing I would ever do. Lady Cowder has put it about that we are to marry, and Kate believes her.'

'But surely you told Kate?'

He shook his head. 'No. There is a great deal that I have to tell Kate, but only at the right moment.' He sat back in his chair. 'And now tell me, how do you feel? All the excitement of your birthday party must have shaken you up a little.'

He drove himself back to London presently, and he thought of Kate every inch of the way.

CHAPTER NINE

MRS CROSBY made an uneventful recovery, and, although Kate was unable to visit her everyday, twice during the following week Briggs took her in the car in the evening when her work was done. She spent her days off in Bath, seeing her mother in the morning and afternoon. Mrs Crosby was out of bed now, walking about, and looking, truth to tell, better than she had done for some weeks—and she listened to Kate's plans with every appearance of interest.

'Mrs Willett is coming back in a week's time,' Kate told her. 'So I shall be leaving very soon now. I've been looking in the local paper; there are several jobs I thought I'd try for. Whichever one I'm lucky enough to get will have somewhere where you and Moggerty and Horace can live with me. Once we're settled I'll go to the bank—there's enough money saved for me to ask them for a loan. Isn't it exciting?'

Her mother agreed, reflecting that Kate didn't look in the least excited—nor did she look happy. The temptation to tell her of Mr Tait-Bouverie's visit was very strong, but she resisted it. Not that he had said much, only that she and Kate weren't to worry about their future.

'I can't think why you're doing this for us,' Mrs Crosby had told him.

He had smiled a little. 'Oh, but I think you can, Mrs

Crosby. If you will leave everything to me...,' he had said.

She had nodded. Before he'd taken his leave of her he had bent and kissed her cheek.

Mr Tait-Bouverie, home late from the hospital, was greeted by Mudd with the promise of dinner within half an hour—and the information that Miss Claudia Travers had telephoned. 'She wishes you to join a few friends at the theatre tomorrow evening, sir, and would you phone her back as soon as you returned.' Mudd managed to sound disapproving. 'I informed her that you would probably be late home.'

'Splendid, Mudd. Come into the study, there's a good fellow...'

Once Mudd was seated opposite him, with the desk between them, Mr Tait-Bouverie said, 'Mudd, the mother of the young lady I intend to marry has been ill. I think it would be a good idea if she were to convalesce at the cottage at Bosham. Mrs Squires sees to the place when we're not there, doesn't she? Do you suppose she would go each day and cook and clean and so on while Mrs Crosby is there? It may be necessary for you to go down from time to time and make sure that everything is as it should be. She will be joined by her daughter very shortly.'

'You won't be going down yourself, sir?'

'Oh, very probably, but I can't always be sure of getting away.'

'You mentioned that you would be getting married,' said Mudd.

'Yes, indeed—once I can persuade Miss Crosby that she wishes to marry me.'

Mudd looked taken aback. Mr Tait-Bouverie had been

the target of numerous young ladies for a number of years,
all of them ready to fall into his lap at the drop of a hat.
Here was a young lady who needed persuading. Mudd
reflected that she must be someone out of the ordinary.
As long as she didn't interfere in his kitchen...

'I shall notify Mrs Squires of your wishes, sir,' said
Mudd. 'If you could give me a date? She will need to
make beds and air the place and get in food.'

'It might be as well if you go down yourself and make
sure that everything is just so, Mudd. Thursday week—
eight days' time.' Mr Tait-Bouverie was lost in thought.
'If I can manage a day off I'll drive you down early in
the morning and leave you there, then go on to Bath and
collect Mrs Crosby, bring her to Bosham and drive you
back here with me.'

'Miss Crosby?' ventured Mudd.

'She won't be free for another day or so. I'll fetch her
then.'

Mudd went away then to prepare the dinner, leaving
Mr Tait-Bouverie sitting there with Prince's great head on
his knee, lost in thought. When the phone rang he lifted
the receiver and heard Claudia's shrill voice. 'James,
didn't you get my message? Why haven't you telephoned
me?'

Mr Tait-Bouverie said smoothly, 'Yes, I had your message, Claudia. I'm afraid that it is a waste of time including me in your social activities—indeed, in any part of
your life. I feel that our lives are hardly compatible. I'm
sure you must agree.' Because he was a kind man he
added, 'I'm sure that you have a host of admirers.'

Claudia snapped, 'Yes, I have, and they're all young
men,' and slammed down the receiver.

Mr Tait-Bouverie put down the phone, quite unmoved
by this reference to his age. 'When I'm seventy,' he told

Prince cheerfully, 'our eldest son will be the age I am now.'

Prince rumbled an answer and blew gently onto his master's hand, waiting patiently for Mudd to come and tell them that dinner was on the table.

Mrs Crosby was to leave hospital the following day and Kate had packed a case of clothes to take to her. Mr Tombs had told her that she might have the time off to take them during the evening. 'But see that you are back in good time,' he had told her. 'One must not take advantage of Mrs Braithewaite's generosity.'

So Kate, carrying the case, got into the car with Briggs and made her way to her mother's room. 'Will you be all right?' she asked Briggs anxiously. 'Where will you wait? I may be half an hour at least...'

'Don't you worry your head, Kate, you come back here when you're ready.'

Her mother was sitting in a small armchair, and it struck Kate that she looked guilty—but she looked excited too.

She kissed her parent and asked, 'What's the paper and pencil for? Are you making lists?' She opened the case. 'I brought your tweed suit and a woolly, and your brown shoes; you won't need a hat. I'll unpack them and leave the case to put your nightie and dressing gown in when I come to fetch you.'

She glanced up, saw her mother smiling at someone behind her and spun round. Mr Tait-Bouverie, immaculate as to person, pleasantly remote as to manner, was standing just inside the door. He shut it quietly and said, 'Hello, Kate.'

Kate said, 'Hello.' And then, 'Why are you here again?'

He put his hands in his trouser pockets and leaned against the door. He looked enormous. 'Your mother is going to convalesce at my cottage at Bosham. She will be well looked after by Mrs Squires, who takes care of the place for me. You will be able to join her as soon as you leave Mrs Braithewaite's.'

Kate stared at him. 'High-handed,' she said at length. 'That's what you are—arranging everything behind my back.' She rounded on her mother. 'You knew about this, but you didn't tell me…'

'Well, darling, it seemed best not to, for I thought you would object.'

'Of course I object. I can take care of you at the cottage…'

'I understand that you will be leaving there within the next few days,' observed Mr Tait-Bouverie pleasantly. 'Have you found somewhere else to go?'

When she didn't answer he added, 'Kate, your mother will need a little while to get absolutely fit. The cottage is empty; a short while there will give you time to find another job. No one will bother you, you can go job hunting knowing that your mother is in good hands.

'I knew that you would dislike the idea simply because it was I who instigated it, but you will see nothing of me. Stay there until you have found something to your liking and move out when you wish to. I am sure that you agree with me that your mother's health is more important than any personal feelings you may have.'

Beneath the pleasant manner was a hint of steel. He had, reflected Kate crossly, managed to make her look selfish. She said stiffly, 'Very well. If you think that is the best thing for Mother, we accept your offer. It is most kind of you, if you're sure that it will be quite convenient? I'll ask for my free day and take Mother to Bosham. But Mr Tombs will want a day's notice, so if Mother could stay here for another day?'

'No need. I'll drive her there myself tomorrow morning, see her safely in and go on back to town. You will be free very shortly, I take it?'

'Yes.' She saw that wasn't going to be enough and added, 'Mrs Willett comes back in two days, and I'm to go three days later.'

Mr Tait-Bouverie, who knew all that already, nodded. 'Splendid.' He went to Mrs Crosby and took her hand. 'I'll be here for you about ten o'clock tomorrow. You've been a model patient.'

He went away quietly with a brief nod to Kate, who watched him go with her heart in her boots. Nothing could have been more polite and thoughtful than his manner towards her—and nothing, she reflected bitterly, could have been so uninterested. She thought fleetingly of Norway—they had been friends then. Of course, he would never understand that it was loving him that made it so difficult to accept his kindness, knowing that he didn't care for her in the least.

Her mother's voice roused her. 'Isn't it marvellous?' she wanted to know. 'It gives us a breathing space, doesn't it, darling? There's just one thing—would you be able to send on some more of my clothes? I've only got one of everything in the case, haven't I? And the nightie and the dressing gown here.'

'I'll ask Mr Briggs to bring me back. If I go home now I can pack a few things and bring them straight here. I'll bring the rest with me when I leave. Mother, what about Horace and Moggerty?'

'Oh, James said he'd deal with that...'

'How, Mother?'

'I've no idea, but if he says he will do something he does it, doesn't he?'

All the same, thought Kate, I'll have to make sure. She

emptied the case, told her mother that she would be back
as soon as possible and sped down to the hospital entrance. Mr Briggs was nowhere to be seen, but Mr Tait-
Bouverie was. He took the case from her, took her arm
and popped her into his car before she had time to utter
a remark.

'Mr Briggs,' she managed. 'I must see him—he's got
to bring me back—Mother's clothes—you don't understand...'

'Briggs has gone home. I'll drive you back and wait
while you pack whatever your mother needs. No need for
you to come back here; I'll see that she gets them.'

She could think of nothing to say as he drove her back.
She would have to apologise; she had been absolutely
beastly to him. If he had been angry it would have been
easier... She tried out one or two suitable speeches in her
head but they didn't sound right—but until she had told
him that she was sorry it was hard to behave with the
same friendliness which he had shown. It would be much
easier if she didn't love him so much...

He went with her to the cottage and sat patiently with
the cats on his knee while she flung things into the case.
As well as clothes she grabbed her mother's modest make-
up, more wool for her knitting, a writing pad and more
shoes. She carried it down to the sitting room and found
him asleep. Somehow the sight of him made it easy; there
was no need for speeches.

'I'm sorry,' she said. 'I've been horrible to you, and
you've shown us nothing but kindness, and I feel awful
about it. I hope you'll forgive me.'

He had opened his eyes and was watching her. He
wasn't smiling, and he looked politely indifferent. He said
coolly, 'You have made such a colossal mountain out of
a molehill that you can't see the wood for the trees, Kate.

Rather a mixed metaphor, but really true.' He got up. 'Is this all that your mother needs? Have you any message for her?'

'No, thank you. There's a note in the case.'

Kate watched him walk to the door. He had said that he wouldn't be going to Bosham while they were there— she wouldn't see him again and he hadn't said that he'd forgiven her, had he? She swallowed back tears and wished him goodbye in a polite voice.

He didn't answer that, but said, 'Don't worry about the cats; some arrangement will be made for them.'

He had gone before she could assure him that she would take them with her when she went.

When she was sure that he had gone she sat down at the table in the kitchen. Horace and Moggerty came and sat with her, and presently she got up and fed them, made a pot of tea, drank it and went to bed. She was still the cook, and had to be up and about by seven o'clock.

Although she was tired she slept badly, but once her day had begun she worked her way through it in her usual calm and unhurried way. It was as they were finishing their midday dinner that Tombs, who had been called away, returned and told her that he had received a telephone call from Mr Tait-Bouverie to say that Mrs Crosby was installed in the cottage at Bosham and was well.

'I have ascertained the telephone number, should you wish to speak to your mother. You may use the kitchen telephone, Kate, after six o'clock.'

It was almost eight o'clock before she found the time to do so. She smiled at the sound of her mother's cheerful voice. It had been a lovely drive to Bosham, said Mrs Crosby, they had stopped and had coffee on the way and the cottage was delightful, and so comfortable. Mrs

Squires had been waiting for them with James's man, Mudd.

'Such a nice person, Kate, and so efficient. I have a lovely room, and Mrs Squires is sleeping here until you come. James and Mudd went off just before tea, back to London. Mudd told me that James has a house there.' Mrs Crosby was bubbling over. 'Kate, he's thought of everything. The local doctor is coming to make sure that I am well, and he's left me his phone number.'

'I'm glad everything is so delightful, Mother. Take care, won't you? I'll be with you in four days. I'll find out the best way to travel. Train to Chichester, I expect, and then a bus...'

'Oh, I dare say,' said Mrs Crosby airily. Much later it struck Kate that her mother had shown very little interest in her journey. It was going to be an awkward one, what with the luggage and the cats...

Mrs Willett, well again and eager to resume her place in the household, took over the cooking from Kate at once. 'You'll need to pack up,' she pointed out. 'I must say you've kept the cottage very nice, and Mr Tombs told me that Mrs Braithewaite was very satisfied with your work.'

Kate replied suitably and, given a free afternoon, began the task of packing the two suitcases she would have to take with her—watched with deep suspicion by Horace and Moggerty, who got into the cases each time she opened them. 'You're coming with me,' she assured them, and wondered where all of them would finally end up. Chichester sounded nice; if they could find a small house there... She would have to go to the bank, too, and if she could get the money she wanted she would begin the slow process of building up the home catering business. Kate sighed. There was a lot to do before she could get started.

'But at least we've saved more money than we expected to,' she told the cats, and if I can get a part-time job to start with...'

The last day came. She was to leave in the early afternoon and take a train from Bath—an awkward journey, but she had worked it out carefully. She had her breakfast, made sure that the cottage was exactly as Mrs Willett wanted it to be, and, bidden by Tombs, went to say goodbye to Mrs Braithewaite.

'You're a good cook,' said that lady. 'They say the way to a man's heart is through his stomach,' she chuckled. 'I wish you well, Kate.'

Kate thanked her. She wanted to point out that it wasn't only men she intended to cater for—birthday parties, family gatherings, even weddings were what she aimed for—but there was no point in saying so. She said goodbye in her quiet manner and went down to the kitchen. They would be having their morning coffee, and she could do with a cup.

So, it seemed, could Mr Tait-Bouverie, sitting there with a mug in one hand and a hunk of cake in the other. He put both down as she went in, watched the surprised delight in her face with deep satisfaction and got to his feet.

'Good morning, Kate. I'll drive you down to Bosham; I'm on my way there now.'

She had wiped the delight from her face and found her voice.

'I've booked a taxi...'

'Tombs has cancelled it. I'll go and say goodbye to my aunt while you have your coffee and then collect your things and the cats from the cottage.'

Mrs Willett chimed in. 'That's right, dear, you sit down

for five minutes. Mr James will let you know when he is ready.'

Kate sat. There really wasn't much else she could do without making a fuss. There would be time enough to tell him what she thought of his high-handed actions once they were in the car.

Once they were on their way, with the cats on the back seat and the luggage in the boot, she found it difficult to begin. She mulled over several tart comments as to his behaviour, but they didn't sound right in her head and would probably come out all wrong if she uttered them.

'I'm waiting,' said Mr Tait-Bouverie.

'Waiting for what?'

'The tart reprimand I feel sure is quivering on your lip. Oh, and quite justified too. I have no business to interfere with your life, I ride roughshod over your plans, I turn up without warning and order you about. I am, in short, a tiresome fellow.'

Which was exactly what she had intended to say herself. She thought how much she loved him even when he annoyed her. He had been kind and helpful and, more than that, they had been friends. He might be going to marry Claudia—although how he could love the girl was something she would never know—but she thought that he liked her...

'Well, you do arrange things, don't you?' she said. 'I mean without saying so, but I expect that's because you're used to doing it at the hospital. I've been ungrateful and snappy. I'm sorry.'

'Good. We understand each other. Try calling me James.'

'No,' said Kate. 'How can I do that when I've cooked dinner for you?'

'Do you mean to tell me that when my wife cooks my dinner she will refuse to call me James?'

'Of course not. This is a silly question.' She added, 'Can Claudia cook?'

'Most unlikely, but Mudd, my man, is capable of that.' She didn't see his smile.

It wasn't any good; she couldn't go on being vexed with him. Anyway, it was a waste of time for he had an answer for everything. Presently she found herself telling him of her plans, comfortably aware that he was listening—indeed, was making helpful suggestions.

She was quietly happy, even though she knew that the happiness wouldn't last. Each time they had met she had told herself that she wouldn't see him again, but there had always been a next time. These few hours together really would be the last. He had said that he wouldn't be going down to the cottage while they were there, and why should he? He had his own busy life and his marriage to plan. Her heart gave a painful twist at the thought.

She was enchanted by Bosham when they reached it, and when he stopped outside the cottage she stuck her head out of the window to take a better look.

'It's yours? It's lovely. Couldn't you live here always? It's not very far to London, is it?'

'No, but it's too far to travel there and back every day. Besides, I have a very pleasant house in London.'

He had got out and opened her door and she stood outside beside him, looking around her. It was, in Kate's opinion, quite large for a cottage, but it had a thatched roof and a number of small windows, and a solid door in a porch. Although summer was long over there were chrysanthemums and late roses, and a firethorn against one wall, vivid scarlet against the grey stone.

The door had opened and Mr Tait-Bouverie took her

arm and urged her up the short path. Mudd was there,
waiting for them, bidding them good day and casting a
sharp eye over Kate. Very nice too, he considered, and
ushered them into the narrow hall.

'Mrs Crosby is in the sitting room,' he informed them.
'Mrs Squires will serve lunch in half an hour, sir. I will
see to the luggage and the cats.'

Mr Tait-Bouverie gave Kate a small shove. 'The sitting
room's there, on the left. Go on in. I'll come presently;
I must speak to Mudd.'

So Kate went in through the half-open door and found
her mother waiting for her.

'Kate, dear. Oh, how lovely to see you. I've not been
lonely for one moment. Mrs Squires is marvellous, and
there's so much to do—and Mudd came this morning, and
Prince too. You're all right? Mrs Braithewaite was pleasant? And the others? And did you have a good trip?'

Kate hugged her mother. 'Mother, you look marvellous.
Are you all right? Was the doctor pleased with you? Are
you eating well and sleeping?'

'Yes to that, my dear. I never felt better. I still get a
bit tired, but that's normal. Another two weeks and I shall
be better than I've been for a long time.'

Kate took off her coat, looking around her. The room
was low-ceilinged and quite large, with a wide hearth with
a brisk fire burning. The walls were cream, and there was
a number of pictures. She would look at those later. The
furniture was exactly right—deep armchairs, a wide sofa
on either side of the hearth, and little lamp-tables—an-
tiques, just as the bow-fronted cabinet against one wall
was antique. There was a beautiful sofa-table with a bowl
of chrysanthemums on it, and a charming little desk in
one corner.

'It's perfect,' said Kate.

Mr Tait-Bouverie came in then, with the cat baskets, and Prince prancing beside him. To Mrs Crosby's expressed worries that Prince would eat the cats up Mr Tait-Bouverie said placidly, 'They'll be quite safe,' and let them out. Prince sat, obedient to his master's quiet voice, while Horace and Moggerty prowled cautiously round the room and presently climbed into a chair and sat, eyeing Prince, who lay down, put his head between his paws and went to sleep.

They drank their sherry, then, and Mrs Crosby and Mr Tait-Bouverie carried on a pleasant conversation about nothing much—and if they noticed that Kate had very little to say they didn't comment upon it.

They had lunch presently, but they didn't linger over it; Mr Tait-Bouverie had to return to London, taking Mudd and Prince with him, so that the cottage seemed suddenly very empty. Kate, watching the car disappear down the lane, reflected that he had said nothing about seeing them again. He had bidden her mother a cheerful goodbye, and when Kate had begun to thank him for driving her down and waved her thanks aside with a brief goodbye which had left her downcast. She deserved it, of course; she had said some awful things to him. She went red just remembering.

The rest of the cottage was just as perfect as the sitting room. Her bedroom wasn't over large, but the bed and the dressing table were dainty Regency, and the curtains and bedspread were pale pink and cream. The pink was echoed in the little armchair by the window and the lamps on either side of the bed. Her mother's room was larger and just as pretty. 'The loveliest room is at the back,' said Mrs Crosby. 'It's large with its own bathroom; I peeped in one day.'

Her mother was happy. After the places they had been

living in, this must remind her of the house she had had
when Kate's father had been alive. Kate would have to
find work quickly and postpone her catering once more;
with a decent job they could afford to live in a better
house. There was the money she had saved—some of it
could be used to pay rent...

'I shall go to Chichester tomorrow,' said Kate. 'And
find an agency.'

'Darling, you've only just got here. James assured me
that there was no hurry for us to leave. It's too late in the
year for him to sail and he has a great deal of work, he
told me.'

'Did he say when he was getting married?' asked Kate
casually.

Her mother hesitated. 'Well, no, dear, not exactly.'

Kate said quickly, 'I'll feed the cats. They seem to have
settled down nicely. Mrs Squires won't mind if I go into
the kitchen?'

'Of course not, Kate. Now you're here, she said she
would just come for a couple of hours in the mornings
and then for an hour or so to see to the dishes after lunch.
She'll be glad not to have to come out in the evening now
it's getting dark early.'

It seemed a suitable arrangement. 'I'll come whenever you
want me,' Mrs Squires told Kate the next day. 'If you're
wanting to go away and don't like to leave your mother,
just you say.'

'Thank you, I might be glad of that. I must go and look
for a job. I thought Chichester...'

'As good a place as any,' said Mrs Squires. 'There's a
good agency in the High Street, and plenty of hotels and
big houses in and around the town.'

Kate didn't go to Chichester. The weather was bright

but chilly, and her mother wanted to explore Bosham. 'I'm quite able to walk,' she declared. 'And it is such a delightful little place. Besides, I want to hear your plans. If you could find somewhere cheap where we could live, you could start cooking...but do you have to go to the bank first?'

Mrs Crosby spoke with an overbright cheerfulness which caused Kate to give her a thoughtful look. Kate had had a wakeful night. She must face the future with common sense and set aside her dreams of starting a catering business. Seeing her mother so happy in the charming little cottage, living the kind of life they had led when her father had been alive, she realised that she must plan and decide on a different future.

She said now, 'There's plenty of time to make plans, and it's a good day for a walk. Shall we go down to the harbour?'

Her mother's face lit up.

They had a very happy day, exploring the little village at their leisure. There weren't many people and they spent a pleasant half-hour having coffee in a small café empty of other customers. 'A bit quiet,' said the owner, 'but it's busy enough at the weekend—they come down to overhaul their boats and do a bit of painting and such. Staying long, are you?'

'A week or so,' said Kate cautiously.

'Very nice it is at Mr Tait-Bouverie's cottage. Keeps it nice, he does, and always has a friendly word. Got a lot of friends here.' She added, 'Mrs Squires is my sister-in-law.'

On the way back Kate said, 'Perhaps we had better be a bit careful what we say in front of Mrs Squires, but I suppose in a small place there's always a bit of gossip.'

That night, lying in bed wide awake, Kate thought

about their future. She discarded the idea of finding work
in Chichester—it was too near the cottage and Bosham,
and there would be the risk of meeting James when he
spent his weekends there. He would have Claudia with
him... She wouldn't be able to bear seeing them together.
She would have to think up a good reason for moving
away where she would never see him again.

Tomorrow, she promised herself, she would get a copy
of *The Lady* and look for a job—preferably in the north
or along the east coast. She would have to give her mother
a good reason for that, too. She could see now that there
would be little chance of her starting up on her own, not
for several years.

Not that it mattered any more—the future unrolled before her with no James in it. She thrust the thought aside
and concentrated on a possible move to a job which would
be suitable. There was her mother to consider, and the
cats. They would need a roof over their heads and a decent
wage. If she abandoned her catering plans there wouldn't
be the need to scrape and scrimp. They would go out
more, buy new clothes—enjoy life!

Having made these suitable arrangements, Kate had a
good cry and fell asleep at last.

She awoke very early and, rather than lie there thinking
of the same unhappy things, she got out of bed and looked
out of the window. It was a grey morning and still not
light. A cup of tea would be nice, and she might go to
sleep again. She didn't wait to put on her dressing gown
but crept barefoot down the stairs and into the kitchen.

Mr Tait-Bouverie was sitting on the kitchen table, the
teapot beside him, a slice of bread and butter in his hand.
He looked up as she paused in the doorway and said,
'Good morning, Kate,' and smiled at her.

Kate's heart beat so loudly and so fast that she thought he must surely hear it. She drew a difficult breath. 'How did you get in?'

He looked surprised. 'I have a key.'

'Is something the matter? Do you want something?'

'Nothing is the matter. I do want something, but that can wait for the moment. Would you like some tea?'

She nodded. 'Yes, please.'

He got up and fetched another mug from the dresser. 'Then run upstairs and get a dressing gown and slippers. You look charming, but you distract me.'

Kate said, 'Oh,' and fled back to her room and wrapped herself tightly in the sensible garment she had had for years. It concealed her completely, and would never wear out. At least it covered the cheap cotton nightie she was wearing.

She went back downstairs, feeling shy. Mr Tait-Bouverie's glance slid over her person with the lack of interest of someone reading yesterday's newspaper, so that she felt instantly comfortable. She sat down by the Aga and, since she longed to look at him, she kept her eyes on Prince, snoozing comfortably between Moggerty and Horace.

Presently she asked the question which had been on the tip of her tongue. 'Is Claudia with you?'

He looked amused. 'No.'

'She knows you are here?'

'No. Why should she?'

'Well, if it was me,' said Kate, throwing grammar to the winds, 'I'd want to know.'

'Well, shall we throw Claudia out of the window, meta-phorically speaking? She's no concern of mine. I can't think why you've dragged her into the conversation.'

'We weren't having a conversation. And how can you

talk like that about her when you are going to marry her?'
She added defiantly, 'Lady Cowder said so.'

'One of my least likeable aunts. I have no intention of
marrying Claudia. I don't like her, Mudd doesn't like her,
Prince doesn't like her...'

'Then why are you here?'

'Because I have something to say to you. On several
occasions I have tried to do so and each time I have been
thwarted. Now you are in my house, in my kitchen, and
I shall speak my mind.'

Kate got up. 'I said I was sorry, and I am. I didn't mean
any of the things I said...'

'Well, of course you didn't.' He had come to stand very
near her, and when she would have taken a prudent step
back he folded his great arms around her, wrapping her
so close that she could feel his heart beating under her
ear.

'I've been in love with you for a very long time now,
my darling, and I have waited for you to discover that
you loved me, too—and that hasn't been easy. Such a
hoity-toity miss, hiding behind her cook's apron...'

'Well, I am a cook,' said Kate into his shirt-front, and
then, because she was an honest girl, she said, 'But I do
love you, James.'

He put a gentle finger under her chin, smiling down at
her. He kissed her then, slowly and with the greatest of
pleasure, for this was the moment he had waited for. Kate
kissed him back and then paused to ask, 'Mother! What
about Mother...?'

'Hush, my love. Your mother and I have had a little
talk. She is happy to live here with Mrs Squires to look
after her. We shall come down whenever I'm free. You
won't mind living in London? I have a house there, a
pleasant place.'

Kate reflected that she would live in a rabbit hutch as long as she was with James. 'It sounds very nice,' she said.

'Oh, it is.' Hardly a good description of the charming little house overlooking the river.

Something in his voice made her ask, 'James, are you rich?'

'I'm afraid so. Don't let it worry you, my love.'

Kate stared up at him. 'No, I won't—it doesn't matter in the least, does it?'

'No.'

'Although, of course…' began Kate.

Mr Tait-Bouverie kissed her silent. 'Will you marry me, Kate?'

'Well, yes—of course I will, James.' She smiled at him. 'Ought we to sit down and discuss it? The wedding and so on?'

'With all the will in the world, my dearest girl, but first of all…'

He bent his head to kiss her, and Kate, in a happy world of her own, kissed him back.

**What happens when you suddenly discover your happy twosome is about to turn into a...*family?*
Do you laugh?
Do you cry?
Or...do you get married?**

The answer is all of the above—and plenty more!

Share the laughter and tears with
Harlequin Romance® as these
unsuspecting couples have to be

When parenthood takes you by surprise!

Authors to look out for include:

**Caroline Anderson—DELIVERED: ONE FAMILY
Barbara McMahon—TEMPORARY FATHER
Grace Green—TWINS INCLUDED!
Liz Fielding—THE BACHELOR'S BABY**

Available wherever Harlequin books are sold.

Visit us at www.eHarlequin.com   HRREADY

From bestselling
Harlequin American Romance author

CATHY GILLEN THACKER

comes

TEXAS VOWS

A McCABE FAMILY SAGA

Sam McCabe had vowed to always
do right by his five boys—but after
the loss of his wife, he needed the small-town security
of his hometown, Laramie, Texas, to live up to that
commitment. Except, coming home would bring him
back to a woman he'd sworn to stay away from.
It will be one vow that Sam can't keep....

On sale March 2001

Available at your favorite retail outlet.

HARLEQUIN®
Makes any time special ™

PHTV

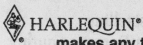

NEARLYWEDS

Almost at the altar—will these *nearlyweds* become *newlyweds*?

Harlequin Romance® is delighted to invite you to some special weddings! Yet these are no ordinary weddings. Our beautiful brides and gorgeous grooms only *nearly* make it to the altar—before fate intervenes.

But the story doesn't end there....
Find out what happens in these tantalizingly emotional novels!

Authors to look out for include:

Leigh Michaels—The Bridal Swap
Liz Fielding—His Runaway Bride
Janelle Denison—The Wedding Secret
Renee Roszel—Finally a Groom
Caroline Anderson—The Impetuous Bride

Available wherever Harlequin books are sold.

HARLEQUIN®
Makes any time special ™